I0631299

S. Sitarama Sastri

Jsa, Kena and Mundaka Upanishads

Vol.1

S. Sitarama Sastri

Jsa, Kena and Mundaka Upanishads
Vol.1

ISBN/EAN: 9783337384869

Printed in Europe, USA, Canada, Australia, Japan

Cover: Foto ©Andreas Hilbeck / pixelio.de

More available books at **www.hansebooks.com**

ओं

सत्यान्नास्तिपरोधर्मः

THE

Isa, Kena & Mundaka
UPANISHADS

AND

SRI SANKARA'S COMMENTARY

TRANSLATED BY

S. SITARAMA SASTRI, B. A.,

PUBLISHED BY

V. C. SESHACHARRI, B. A., B. L.,

Vakil, High Court, Madras.

FIRST VOLUME.

Madras:

G. A NATESAN & CO., PRINTERS & PUBLISHERS, ESPLANADE.

1898.

DEDICATED

BY KIND PERMISSION

TO

Mrs. Annie Besant.

CONTENTS.

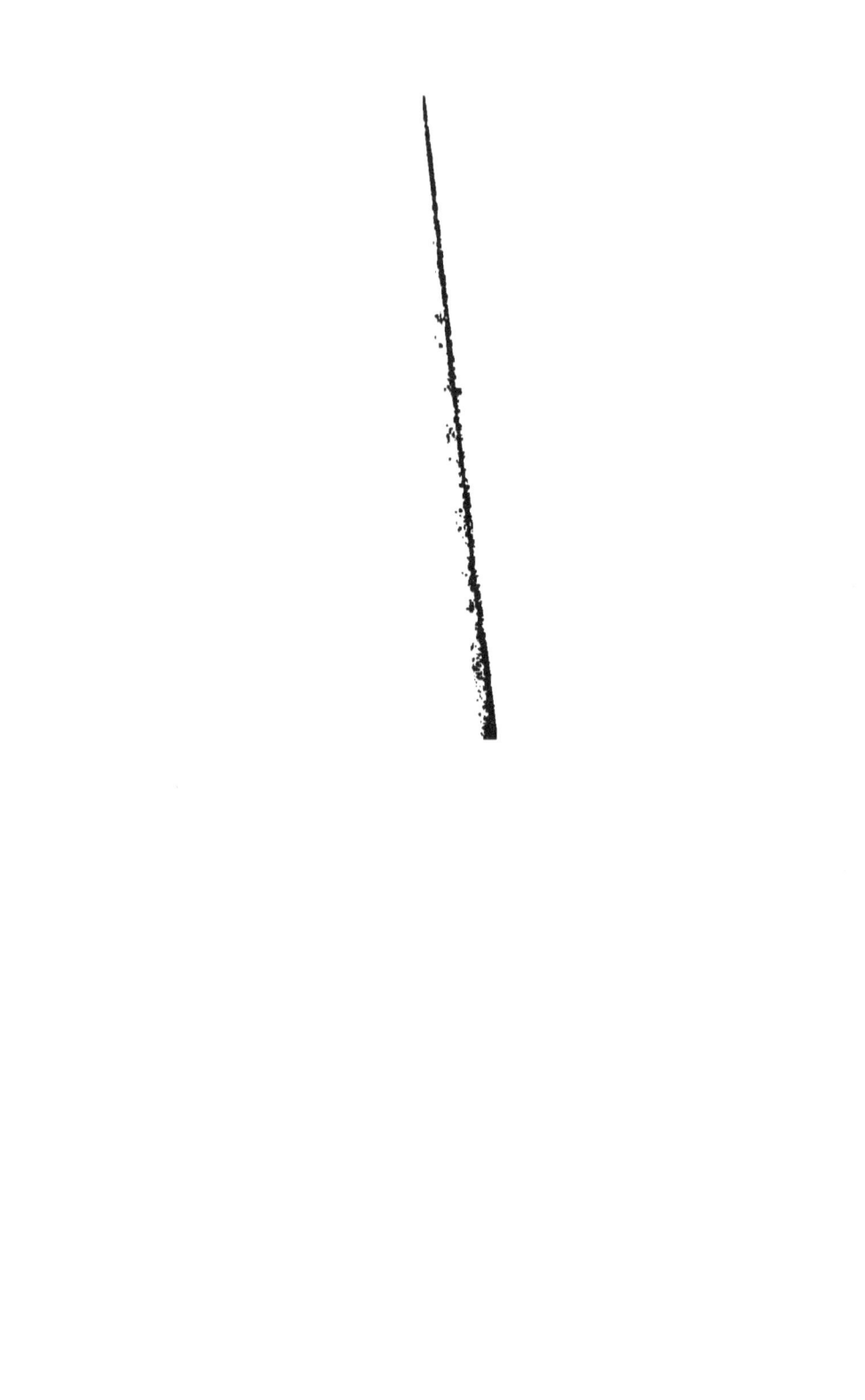

PREFACE.

The increasing interest evinced by the thinking world in the Philosophy and Religion of the Hindus has led me to undertake the publication of the translation of the principal Upanishads.

The special feature of this publication is the translation of the commentary of Sri Sankaracharya, the greatest exponent of the Advaita system of philosophy.

The work has been undertaken chiefly with a view to bring within easy reach of the English-reading public the priceless teachings of the Upanishads, in the light of the interpretation of Sri Sankaracharya.

The spirit of the text and of the interpretation has throughout been faithfully adhered to and, perhaps, in some instances, even to the detriment of elegance in diction.

If the earnest student finds any the least help from this work, the publication will be amply justified.

My hearty thanks are due to Mr. V. Swaminatha Iyer. District Munsiff, for the care with which he went through the translation and for his many valuable suggestions.

MADRAS.   V. C. SESHACHARRI.
February 1898.   *Publisher.*

Isavasyopanishad.

Sri Sankara's Introduction.

OM TAT SAT.

Adoration to the Brahman. The mantras beginning
with Isavasyam, etc., have not been utilized in rituals,
because they serve the purpose of enlightening us on
the true nature of the Atman who is not an *anga* of,
i. e., not connected with, Karma. The true nature of
the Atman consists, as will be described, in its purity,
being untouched by sin, oneness, being eternal, having
no body, omnipresence, etc., and as that conflicts with
Karma, it is only reasonable that these mantras should
not be utilized in rituals ; nor is the true nature of
the Atman thus defined, a product, a modification, a
thing to be attained or a thing to be refined; nor is
it of the nature of a doer or enjoyer so that it may be
connected with Karma. All the Upanishads exhaust
themselves in describing the true nature of the Atman ;
and the Gita and the Mokshadharma are bent on the
same end. Therefore all Karma has been enjoined

in accordance with worldly understanding, which attributes to the Atman diversity, agency, enjoyment,
impurity, sinfulness, etc. Those that know who are
competent to perform Karma and who are not,
(Adhikaravidah) tell us that he who seeks the fruits of
Karma—visible such as the inherent splendour of a
Brahmin and invisible such as Heaven, etc.,—and thinks
"I am a twice-born free from any defect such as being
one-eyed or hunch-backed, &c. which disqualifies one
for the performance of Karma" is entitled to perform Karma. So, these mantras by enlightening (us)
on the true nature of the Atman remove our natural
ignorance and produce in us the knowledge of the
oneness, etc. of the Atman,—the means of uprooting grief, delusion, etc. the concomitants of *Samsara*.
We shall now briefly comment upon the mantras, the
persons competent to study which, the subject matter
of which, the relevancy of which (Sambandha) and the
fruits of which, have been thus declared.

ओं। पूर्णमदः पूर्णमिदं पूर्णात्पूर्णमुदच्यते ।
पूर्णस्य पूर्णमादाय पूर्णमेवावशिष्यते ॥

The whole (Brahman) is all that is invisible. The
whole (Brahman) is all that is visible. The whole
(Hiranyagarbha) was born out of the whole (Brahman).
When the whole (the Universe) is absorbed into the

whole (Brahman) the whole alone (Brahman) remains.
Om. Peace! Peace!! Peace!!!

ईशावास्यमिद ५ सर्वं यत्किञ्च जगत्यां जगत् ।
तेन त्यक्तेन भुञ्जीथा मा गृधः कस्य स्विद्धनम् ॥ १ ॥

All this—whatsoever moveth on the earth—should
be covered by the Lord. That renounced, enjoy.
Covet not anybody's wealth.

Commentary.—The word 'Isa' is from the verb '*Ishte*'
(rules) and means 'by the Lord.' The Lord is Para-
meswara, the Paramatman of all. He rules everything
being the Atman of all. Should be covered by the
Lord, by his own self, the Atman. What? All this,
whatsoever moveth on the earth. All this universe,
movable and immovable, unreal in absolute truth,
should be covered by his self, the Lord, Paramatman,
with the idea, "I alone am all this as being the
inner self of all." Just as the bad odour—the result
of moisture, etc.—produced by contact with water, in
sandal and agaru, etc., is hidden (lost) in their naturally
agreeable smell produced by the process of rubbing,
similarly all this on this earth (the word *earth* being illustratively used for the whole Cosmos) differentiated
as name, form, and action, this bundle of modifications,
superimposed upon the Atman by ignorance, and consisting in this seeming duality with its distinctions of

doer, enjoyer, etc., will be abandoned by the contemplation of the true Atman. One who thus contemplates
on the self as the Paramatman is bound to renounce the
three-fold desire of son, etc., and not to perform Karma.
' *Tena Tyaktena* ' means ' by such renunciation.' It is
well known that one's son or servant, abandoned
or dead, having therefore no bond of connection,
does not protect that one. 'Renunciation' therefore,
is the meaning of this word *Tyaktena*. *Bhunjithah*
means *protect*. Having thus renounced all desires, do
not cherish any desire for wealth. '*Anybody's wealth* ';
do not long for wealth either yours or another's. *Svit*
is a meaningless particle.

Or it may be thus interpreted. Do not covet. Why ?
' Whose is wealth ?' is used in the sense of an objection ; for nobody has any wealth which could be coveted.
The meaning is "all this has been renounced by the
contemplation of Iswara, that the Atman is all. All
this therefore belongs to the Atman and the Atman
is all. Do not therefore covet what is unreal."

कुर्वन्नेवेह कर्माणि जिजीविषेच्छतꣳसमा: ।
एवं त्वयि नान्यथेतोऽस्ति न कर्म लिप्यते नरे ॥ २ ॥

Should one wish to live a hundred years on this
earth, he should live doing Karma. While thus, (as)
man, you live, there is no way other than this by

which Karma will not cling to you.

Commentary.—Thus the drift of the Vedic text is that he who knows the Atman should renounce the three-fold desire of son, etc., and save his Atman by being centred in the knowledge of the Atman (*Gnana-nishtha*). The Mantras now proceed to inculcate the following for the benefit of him who does not know the Atman and is not competent to cognize the Atman as above indicated.

Kurvannava means 'certainly doing,' *i.e.*, 'only by doing.' *Karmani* means 'Agnihotra, etc.' *Jijirishet* means 'should like to live.' *Satamsamah* means ' a hundred years.' It has been declared that that is a man's longest life. Thus declaring agreeably to natural inclination the desire to live a hundred years, the text lays down the injunction in respect of how one should live—continually performing Karma and not otherwise. If you would thus live, content to be a man, there is no other mode of life than the one of performing Agnihotra, etc., by which bad Karma may not cling to you. Therefore, one should like to live doing Karma enjoined by the Sastras such as Agnihotra, etc. But how is this drift arrived at ? By the previous *mantra*, Gnananishtha has been inculcated to the sanyasin. By this, Karmanishtha is enjoined on those who are not able to become sanyasins. Do you not remember it was pointed out that the antithesis between Knowledge and Karma is a fact unshakable like a mountain? Here also it has been said that he who *would like to live* must perform Karma and that this universe must be abandoned as unreal in the contemplation of the Lord as all, by one who would protect his Atman having renounced all and not coveting anybody's wealth. According to the Srutis it is settled that one should not long for either life or death and should leave for the forest. There is also the injunction by which one is interdicted from returning thence—thus ordaining sanyasa. The distinction in the results of the two courses will also be pointed out. (The Narayana Upanishad) says, "In the beginning these two roads were laid. The road through Karma and Sanyasa; the latter consists in the renunciation of the three-fold desire. Of these, the road through Sanyasa is the preferable one." The Taitiriya Upanishad also says, " Renunciation (Nyasa) certainly is to be preferred."

Bhagavan Vyasa, the preceptor of the Vedas, after much discussion told his son his firm conviction in the following text. "These then are the two roads on which the Vedas are based. Both the courses—one which leads to Karma and the other which draws away from Karma have been explained, etc." This division will be explained.

असुर्या नाम ते लोका अन्धेन तमसाऽऽवृताः ।
ता ५ स्ते प्रेत्याभिगच्छन्ति ये के चात्महनो जनाः ॥ ३ ॥

Those births partake of the nature of the Asuras and are enveloped in blind darkness. After leaving the body they who kill their Atman attain them.

Commentary.—This Mantra is begun for the purpose of condemning those who have no knowledge of the Atman. *Asuryah*; even Devas, etc., are Asuras relatively to becoming one with the Paramatman. *Asuryah* because they belong to them (Asuras). *Nama* is a meaningless word. Those *lokas* (births) so called because the fruits of Karma are there perceived or enjoyed (*lokyante*). *Andhena Tamasa*, 'ignorance which consists in inability to see one's self.' *Avritah* means *covered*. These births down to the immoveable. *Pretya* means 'leaving the body.' '*Abhigachchhanthi*' means 'attain in accordance with their Karma and Knowledge.' '*Atmahanah*' means 'those who kill the Atman.' Who are they? Those who do not know the Atman. How do they *kill* the *eternal* Atman? By drawing the veil of ignorance over the Atman that exists. Those who do not, under the influence of their natural tendencies (Prakriti), know the Atman are called 'Atmahanah' (Slayers of the Atman); because in their case the result of the existence of the Atman, *i. e.*, the knowledge of its undecaying and immortal nature is veiled as if the Atman were killed. By this fault of slaying the Atman they get into *Samsara*.

अनेजदेकं मनसो जवीयो नैनदेवा आप्नुवन्पूर्वमर्षत् ।
तद्धावतोऽन्यानत्येति तिष्ठत्तस्मिन्नपो मातरिश्वा दधाति ॥ ४ ॥

It is motionless, one, faster than mind; and the Devas (the senses) could not overtake it which ran before. Sitting, it goes faster than those who run after it. By it, the all-pervading air (Sutratman) supports the activity of all living beings.

Commentary.—As the ignorant by killing their Atman whirl in Samsara, contrariwise, those who know the Atman, attain emancipation; and they are not slayers of the Atman. What then is the nature of the Atman will now be explained.

Anejat is a compound of *na* and *ejat*. The root *eji* means *to shake*. Shaking is motion, *i. e.*, deviation from a fixed position. Free from that, *i. e.*, ever constant. It is, besides, one in all Bhutas. It is fleeter than mind whose characteristics are volition, etc. How is this inconsistent statement made *i. e.*, that it is constant and motionless and at the same time fleeter than mind? This is no fault. This is possible with reference to its being thought of as unconditioned and conditioned. It is constant and motionless in

its unconditioned state. That the mind travels fastest
is well-known to all, seeing that the mind encased
within the body and characterised by volition and
doubt is able at one volition to travel to such distant
places as the Brahmaloka, etc.; and travelling so fast as
it does, it perceives on landing (at its destination) that
the intelligent Atman has, as it were, gone there before
it; therefore, the Atman is said to be fleeter than mind.
Devas, from the root which means 'enlighten,' signifies
the senses such as the eye, etc. *Etat* means the entity
of the Atman which is now being treated of. These
senses could not overtake it. The mind is faster than
these because these are distanced by the activity of the
mind. Not even the semblance of the Atman is
within the perception of the senses; for it had gone
even before the mind which is fleeter than they, being
all-pervading, like the *Akas*. The entity of the Atman,
all-pervading, devoid of any attributes of Samsara, and
in its unconditioned state subject to no modification,
appears to undergo all the changes of Samsara super-
posed upon it, and though one, appears, in the eyes of
ignorant men, diverse and enclosed in every body. It
seems to travel beyond the reach of others' mind, speech,
the senses, &c., which are dissimilar to the Atman,
though they run fast. The sense of '*seems*' is suggested by the mantra using *Tishthat* (sitting). '*Sitting*'

means 'being itself inactive.' 'Tasmin' means 'while
the entity of the Atman endures.' 'Matarisva' means
'air', so called, becouso it moves (Svayati) in
space (Matari—Antariksh6). Air (Motarisvo) is that
whose activity sustains all life, on which all causes
and effects depend, ond in which all theso inhere,
which is called Sutra (thread, as it were) supporting
all tho worlds through which it runs. Tho word
'Apoh' means all Karma—tho manifested activity of
all living things. (This oir) allots to firo, sun, clouds,
&c., their severol functions of flaming, burning, shining, raining, &c. Or it may bo said that it supports
these, from the Srutis, such as " From fear of this, tho
wind blows, &c. " The meoning is thot all these modifications of effects and couses take place only while tho
eternally intelligent entity of tho Atman, the sourco
of all, endures.

तदेजति तन्नेजति तद्दूरे तद्वान्तिके ।
तदन्तरस्य सर्वस्य तदु सर्वस्यास्य बाह्यतः ॥ ५ ॥

It moves, it is motionless. It is distant, it is near.
It is within all, it is without all this.   ·

Commentary.—Showing thot there is no superfluity
of montras, tho following mantra declares again what
was expressed by the previous mantra. 'It' means 'the
entity of the Atman whioh is being treated of.' 'Ejati'

means 'moves.' 'Naijati' means 'does not move of itself.'
The meaning is that though motionless in itself, it *seems*
to move. Besides, it is distant, *i.e.*, it seems to be far
removed, because it is not attainable by the ignorant,
even in the course of hundreds of millions of ages.
Tadvantike is split into *tad, u* and *antike*. It is very
near to the knowing; for it is their Atman. It is not
merely distant and near; it is within everything according to the Sruti "The Atman which is within everything." *All* means 'all the world of names and forms
and activity.' It is without all this, being all-pervading
like the Akas; and within everything, being extremely
subtle. It is indivisible according to the Sruti "It is
dense with knowledge."

यस्तु सर्वाणि भूतान्यात्मन्येवानुपश्यति ।
सर्वभूतेषु चात्मानं ततो न विजुगुप्सते ॥ ६ ॥

Who sees everything in his Atman and his Atman
in everything, by that he feels no revulsion.

Commentary.—Who, *i.e.*, the *Sanyasin*, who wishes for emancipation. All Bhutas, *i.e.*, from the Avyakta
down to the immoveable creation. 'Seeing them all
in his own Atman' means 'seeing that they are not
distinct from his own self.' 'Seeing his Atman in
them all' means. 'seeing his Atman as the Atman of

all.' Just as he finds his Atman the witness of all his perceptions, the thinking principle, pure and unconditioned, the soul of his body, which is a bundle of effects and causes, he finds his Atman in the same unconditioned state, the life principle of all the universe, from the Avyakta down to the immoveable. He who thus views does not turn with revulsion by reason of such view. This statement is only a declaration of a truth already known. All revulsion arises only when one sees anything bad distinct from one's Atman. To one who sees his pure Atman alone continuous, there is no other object which could excite the feeling of revulsion. Therefore he does not turn with revulsion.

यस्मिन्सर्वाणि भूतान्यात्मैवाभूद्विजानतः ।
तत्र को मोहः कः शोक एकत्वमनुपश्यतः ॥ ७ ॥

When to the knower all Bhutas become one with his own Atman, what perplexity, what grief, is there when he sees this oneness.

Commentary.—This other text also expresses the same purport. The word 'Yasmin' means either 'when' or 'in which Atman.' When all the Bhutas have become one with the Atman, owing to the knowledge of the Atman, then or in the case of the Atman, how can there be perplexity or grief? Perplexity and grief, the seed of all desire and Karma, affect the ignorant, but

not him who sees the oneness, pure and like the sky.
The negation of perplexity and grief—the effect of
ignorance—being shown by the form of a question,
the total uprooting of all Samsara with its seed has
been indicated.

स पर्यगाच्छुक्रमकायमव्रणमस्नाविरं ५ शुद्धमपापविद्धम् ।
कविर्मनीषी परिभूः स्वयम्भूर्याथातथ्यतोऽर्थान्व्यदधाच्छाश्वतीभ्यः
समाभ्यः ॥ ८ ॥

He pervaded all, resplendent, bodiless, scatheless,
having no muscles, pure, untouched by sin; far-seeing,
omniscient, transcendent, self-sprung, (he) duly allotted to the various eternal creators their respective
functions.

Commentary.—This text describes the real nature of
the Atman, spoken of in the previous texts. *Sah*
means 'the Atman previously spoken of.' 'Paryagat'
means 'went round.' The meaning is 'he is all-pervading like the Akas.' *Sukram* means pure, hence
bright, resplendent. *Akayam* means 'bodiless,' i. e.,
having no *linga sarira* or subtle body. *Avranam*
means 'scatheless.' 'Asnaviram' means 'having no
muscles.' The adjuncts *Avranam* and *Asnaviram* show
that the Atman has no *sthula sarira* or gross body.
By the word *Suddha*, pure or free from the taint of ig-

noranco, it is shown that it has no *karana sarira* or causal body. 'Apapaviddham' means 'untouched by Karma, good or bad.' 'Sukram' and tho following epithets are to be read as masculine, because of tho beginning and the end being in tho masculino, as *Sah, Kavih,* etc. *Kavih* means far-seeing, *i.e.,* all-seeing; for, says tho Sruti "There is no seer other than the Atman, etc." 'Manishi' means 'prompting tho mind,' hence 'omniscient, omnipotent.' *Paribhuh* means 'being above all.' *Swayambhuh* means 'himself being all abovo and all below becomes all.' Ho, tho ever froe, and omnipotent, being omniscient, allotted their respective functions, *i.e.,* objects to be created to the various and eternal Prajapatis, known popularly as 'years' as aids to tho enjoyment of the fruits of Karma.

अन्धन्तमः प्रविशन्ति येऽविद्यामुपासते ।

ततो भूय इव ते तमोय उ विद्याया ५रताः ॥ ९ ॥

They who worship Avidya alone fall into blind darkness; and they who worship Vidya alono fall into evon greater darkness.

Commentary.—The first purport of the Vedas, tho acquisition of knowledge of the Brahman by renunciation of all desires has been explained in tho first mantra Isavasyam, etc. The second alternative, *i.e.,* tho spending of life in continually performing Karma has been explained, for the benefit of the ignorant who are not capable of Gnananishtha, in the second mantra beginning with 'Kurvanneveha Karmani.' This bifurcation, i.e., Knowledge and Karma here pointed out by these texts has also been clearly indicated in the Brihadaranya Upanishad, by the text "he wished, let me have a wife, etc." And from the texts 'Karma for the ignorant and men having desires' and 'The mind is his Atman and speech, his wife, etc.,' it is clear that ignorance and desires are the characteristics of one engaged in the performance of Karma. Thus, the result of Karma is the creation of the seven kinds of food and of an identification of self with them considered as the Atman. It has also been shown that concentration in the self, i.e., the Atman (as opposed to the performance of Karma) by the renunciation of the three-fold desire of wife, etc., is the only necessary condition for those who know the Atman. Indirectly by condemning the ignorant, the true nature of the Atman has been disclosed to those Sanyasins bent on the acquisition of knowledge by the text beginning with 'Asuryanama' and ending with 'Saparyagat', etc., so as to show that they alone and not those who have desires are qualified to acquire knowledge. To the same effect says the Svetasvatara Upanishad "In the midst of a crowd of seers he taught the greatest and the holiest

truth *to those who belonged to the highest order of life.*"
This text "Andhamtamah," etc., is addressed to those
who desire to live here continually performing Karma.
How is it inferred that this text is addressed to such
only and not to all alike? Because, he who has no desires has got over the false distinction between means
and ends, according to the mantra "Yasmin Sarvani
Bhutani, etc."; for it is easy to perceive that none who
is not a fool will like to associate the knowledge of
unity of the Atman with Karma or with any other
piece of knowledge. But here, in view to combining
two elements, the ignorant are ridiculed. That which
can possibly combine with another, either from logic or
from the Sastras, is here pointed out. It is the knowledge of the deities that is here represented as fit to
combine with Karma, not the knowledge of the Paramatman; for a distinct result is predicated of the
knowledge of the deities by the text 'By such knowledge, the Devaloka is attained.' Either of such knowledge and Karma separately pursued is here denounced,
*not really to condemn but in view to the desirability of
their combination*; for distinct fruits are said to result
from either individually, by the texts " By such knowledge, they climb up to it," " By such knowledge is
Devaloka attained," " There they do not go who go
south " and " By Karma is the abode of the manes

attained." It is also well-known that nothing ordained
by the Sastras can ever become unworthy of performance.

Here, They enter into blind darkness. Who?
They who follow Avidya. Avidya is something other
than Vidya or knowledge, hence Karma; for Karma is
opposed to knowledge. The drift is that those who
are continually performing Agnihotra etc. alone, fall
into darkness. And they fall even into greater darkness. Who? Those who having given up Karma are
always bent upon acquiring the knowledge of the deities. Reason is given for combining Knowledge and
Karma each of which separately bears different fruits.
If one of the two alone bore fruit and the other not,
then by a well-recognised law that which bore no fruit
by itself would become a mere appendage to the other.

अन्यदेवाहुर्विद्ययाऽन्यदाहुरविद्यया ।
इति शुश्रुम धीराणां ये नस्तद्विचचक्षिरे ॥ १० ॥

One result is predicated of Vidya and another of
Avidya. We have so heard from wise men who taught
us both Vidya and Avidya.

Commentary.—'Anyat' means 'something distinct.'
They say that by Vidya, some distinct result is
produced according to the Srutis, "By knowledge is
Devaloka attained" and " By knowledge they climb up

to it." They say that other results are produced by
Avidya (Karma) according to the text " By Karma is
the abode of the manes attained." We have heard this
stated to us by wise men, i.e., those preceptors who
taught us both Knowledge and Karma. The purport is
that this is their view as handed down from preceptor
to disciple.

विद्यां चाविद्यां च यस्तद्वेदोभयꣳ सह ।

अविद्यया मृत्युं तीर्त्वा विद्ययाऽमृतमश्नुते ॥ ११ ॥

He who simultaneously knows both Vidya and Avidya gets over *death* by Avidya and attains *immortality*
by Vidya.

Commentary.—This being so, the following results.
Vidya is the knowledge of the deities; Avidya is
Karma. Who knows that both these should simultaneously be followed by the same person, he alone, so
combining the two, *gradually* secures the one desirable
end. ' By Avidya' means 'by Karma such as Agnihotra,
etc.' 'Death' means 'action and knowledge induced
by Prakriti (nature).' 'Tirtva' means 'having got
over.' 'By Vidya' means 'by the knowledge of the
deities.' 'Asnute' means 'attains.' To become one with
the deities is what is called immortality (Amritam.)

अन्धं तमः प्रविशन्ति येऽसंभूतिमुपासते ।
ततो भूय इव ते तमो य उ संभूत्या ꣡रताः ॥ १२ ॥

They fall into blind darkness who worship the unborn Prakriti. They fall into greater darkness who are
bent upon the Karya Brahman Hiranyagarbha.

Commentary.—Now, in view to the combining of the
worship of the Avyakrita (Prakriti) and manifested
Brahman, each in itself is denounced. " Asambhutih" is
what is not Sambhutih or that which is born of another ;
hence unborn Prakriti. This again is ignorance, cause
of all, known as Avyakrita. Those who worship this
Prakriti, known as Avyakrita, ignorance which is the
cause of all, the seed of all desire and Karma, and mere
blindness in its nature fall into corresponding or answering darkness which is blindness in its nature ; and
they who worship the Karya Brahman named Hiranyagarbha fall into even greater darkness.

अन्यदेवाहुः संभवादन्यदाहुरसंभवात् ।
इति शुश्रुम धीराणां ये नस्तद्विचचक्षिरे ॥ १३ ॥

They say one thing results from the worship of
Hiranyagarbha and another from the worship of Prakriti. We have thus heard it stated by wise preceptors
who taught us that.

Commentary.—Now the distinction in the fruits of

the two individual worships is pointed out in view
to their combination. They have said that from the
worship of Sambhuti or Karya Brahman or Hiranyagarbha results the attainment of Anima and other
Siddhis. Similarly, they have said that according to
Pouranikas the absorption into Prakriti results from the
worship of the unborn Prakriti. We have heard it
thus stated by wise preceptors who taught us the fruits
of the worship of Prakriti and Hiranyagarbha individually.

संभूतिं च विनाशं च यस्तद्वेदोभय ᳵसह ।
विनाशेन मृत्युं तीर्त्वा संभूत्यामृतमश्नुते ॥ १४ ॥

Those who worship the unmanifested Prakriti and
Hiranyagarbha (Destruction) together, get over death
through the worship of Hiranyagarbha and attain
immortality through the worship of Prakriti.

Commentary.—As this is so, this mantra declares the
desirability of combining the worship of Prakriti and
Hiranyagarbha as they combine to secure the one aim
of the individual. 'Vinasa' means that active object
whose characteristic attribute is Destruction, the abstract
being here used for the concrete. 'By *vinasa*'
means 'by the worship of Hiranyagarbha.' 'Gets
over death' means 'gets over the defects of vice,
desires and *anaisvaryam* (limited powers) and at-

tains *anima* and other *siddhis* which are the result of
the worship of Hiranyagarbha. Having thus overcome
anaisvaryam, death, etc., he, by the worship of Prakriti,
attains immortality, *i. e.*, absorption into Prakriti. It
should be noted that the word *Sambhuti* is an apheresis
for *Asambhuti* agreeably to the results predicated, *i. e.*,
absorption into Prakriti.

हिरण्मयेन पात्रेण सत्यस्यापिहितं मुखम् ।
तत्त्वं पूषन्नपावृणु सत्यधर्माय दृष्टये ॥ १५ ॥

The entrance of the True is covered as if by a
golden vessel. Remove, O Sun, the covering that I who
have been worshipping "The True" may behold it.

Commentary.—The highest result that could be
achieved, according to the Sastras, by wealth of men
and the deities is absorption into Prakriti. Up to this
is rotation in Samsara. Beyond this is the result of
the pursuit of knowledge preceded by a renunciation
of all desire, *i. e.*, the seeing of the Atman in everything as indicated in verse 7. Thus the two-fold purport of the Vedas, one stimulating to activity and
the other drawing to renunciation has been explained.
The Bramhanas up to *Prarargya* Brahmana were utilized for the elucidation of the former purport of the
Vedas which is indicated by mandatory and prohibitory
injunctions. The Brihadaranyaka hereafter is to deal

with the elucidation of the latter purport of tho Vedas—renunciation. Now, by what road he, who has been performing Karma as enjoined from conception to the grave and along with it the worship of the lower Brahman in accordance with verse 11, attains immortality, will be explained. He who has been worshipping tho manifested Brahman referred to in the passage " That is the True, the Aditya, the Purusha in this orb; and the Purusha in the left eye ; both these are true " and also has been performing Karma as enjoined, entreats, when tho hour of death is arrived, tho way leading to the Atman—the True, by the text beginning with ' Hiranmayena, etc.' 'Hiranmaya' means seeming golden, hence resplendent. ' Patrena ' means as if by a lid forming a cover. ' Satyasya ' means ' of the Brahman sitting in the orb of the Sun.' 'Apihitam' means 'covered.' 'Mukham' means ' opening.' ' Apavrinu ' means ' open.' ' Satyadharmaya,' ' to me who have been worshipping *Satya* or tho True or who have been practising *satya*, i. e., virtue as enjoined.' ' Drishtaye ' means ' for realizing the Satya or the True which thou art.'

पूषन्नेकर्षे यम सूर्य प्राजापत्य व्यूह रदमीन्समूह ।
तेजो यत्ते रूपं कल्याणतमं तत्ते पश्यामि योऽसावसौ पुरुष:
सोऽहमस्मि ॥ १६ ॥

O Sun, solo traveller of tho Heavens, controller of all, Surya, son of Prajapati, remove thy rays and gather up thy burning light. I behold thy glorious form; I am ho, tho Purusho within thee.

Commentary.—'Pushan,' vocative case meaning 'O Sun.' The Sun is called *Pushan* because he feeds the world. 'Ekarshi' means 'ono who travels alone.' Tho Sun is called Yama, because ho controls all. Ho is called Surya because he imbibes Prana, rays and liquids. 'Prajapatya' means 'son of Prajapati.' 'Vyuha' means 'remove to a distance thy rays.' 'Samuha, means 'gather up, *i. e.*, contract.' 'Tejah' means, 'burning light.' I wish to behold by thy grace thy most glorious form. Moreover I do not entreat thee like a servant. I am he the Purusha within the solar orb, composed of Vyahritis as limbs or parts. 'Purusha' because he has the figure of a man or because he pervades tho whole in the form of Prana and intelligence or because he occupies the city (of tho Soul) *i.e.*, body.

वायुरनिलममृतमथेदं भस्मान्त ५शरीर ।
ओं । क्रतो स्मर कृत ५स्मर क्रतो स्मर कृत ५स्मर ॥१७॥

(Let my) Prana melt into tho all-pervading Air, the eternal Sutratman; and let this body be burnt by fire to ashes; Om. O mind, remember, remember my deeds; O mind, remember, remember my deeds.

Commentary.—Now, as I am dying, let my Prana leave its confinement within this body and join the all-pervading godly form of Air, *i.e.*, the Sutrat-man. The word 'reach' should be supplied to complete the sentence. The idea 'Let my *Linga Sarira* or subtle body purified by knowledge and Karma ascend' must be supplied in virtue of the fact of the speaker entreating a passage. Let this body given as an obla-tion to the fire be reduced to ashes. Om, according to the forms of worship being a *pratika* (substitute) of the nature of the True and called Agni is mentioned as the same as Bramhan. 'Krato,' vocative case, mean-ing 'O mind whose characteristic is volition,' 'Re-member' *i. e.*, the time has come for me to remember what I should. Remember all that I have till now *thought of* 'O Agni, remember what I have *done*' *i.e.*, remember all Karma which I have done from childhood. The repetition of the same words 'Krito Smara' &c., expresses solicitude.

अग्ने नय सुपथा राये अस्मान्विश्वानि देव वयुनानि विद्वान् ।
युयोध्यस्मज्जुहुराणमेनो भूयिष्ठां ते नमउक्तिं विधेम ॥ १८ ॥

O Agni, lead us by the good path to the enjoyment of the fruits of our deeds, knowing O God, all our deeds. Remove the sin of deceit from within us. We offer thee many prostrations by word of mouth.

Commentary.—He requests passage again by another mantra. *Naya* means 'lead.' 'Supatha' means 'by good path.' The attribute in Supatha is used for the purpose of avoiding the southern route. The suppliant seems to say "I have been afflicted by going to and fro by the southern route by which one goes only to return. I therefore entreat you to take me by the good road through which there is no going and returning." 'Rayo' means "to wealth; *i. e.*, to the enjoyment of the fruits of our Karma.' 'Asman' means 'us,' possessed of the fruits of the virtue aforesaid. 'Visvani' means 'all.' O God, 'Vayunani' means 'deeds or knowledge, 'Vidvan' means 'Knowing.' Besides do this : 'Yuyodhi' means 'destroy.' 'Asmat' means 'from us.' 'Juhuranam' means 'consisting in deceit.' 'Enah' means 'sin.' The meaning is :—Thus purified they' could attain what they wish for. "But we are now unable to do you active service. We have to content ourselves by offering you many prostrations."

Now a doubt is raised by some about the construction of the latter halves of mantras 11 and 14. We shall therefore enter into a brief discussion to solve the doubt. What the question is due to shall first be stated. It is, why not understand the term *Vidya* in those passages in its primary sense of 'the knowledge of the Paramatman,' and so Amritatvam ? They argue

4

thus: granted that the knowledge of the Paramatman and the performance of Karma are mutually antagonistic and cannot therefore co-exist, this antagonism is not perceivable; for agreement and antagonism rest alike on the authority of the Sastras. Just as the performance of Karma and the acquisition of Knowledge are matters exclusively based on the Sastras, so also must be the question of their agreement or opposition. Thus we find that the prohibitory injunction 'Do not kill any living thing' is overridden by another Sastraic injunction 'Kill a sheep in a sacrifice.' The same may apply to Karma and Knowledge. If from the text "They are opposed and travel different roads, Knowledge and Karma," it is urged that they cannot co-exist, we say that from the text "He who follows both Knowledge and Karma etc," there is no antagonism between them. We answer that cannot be; for they are opposed to each other in regard to their causes, nature and results. But if it be urged that from the impossibility of Knowledge and Karma being opposed and not opposed to each other and from the injunction to combine them there is no antagonism between them, that is unsound; for their co-existence is impossible. If it be argued that they may gradually grow to co-exist, it is untenable; for when Knowledge arises, Karma cannot exist in the individual to whom Knowledge adheres. It is well known that when one knows that fire is hot and bright he cannot at the same time think that fire is neither hot nor bright or even entertain a doubt as to whether fire is bright or hot; for according to the text " When to the knower all living things become one with his own Atman, where is grief or perplexity to one who sees this unity," grief or perplexity is ont of the question. We have already said that where ignorance ceases its result, Karma, also ceases. The *immortality* in ' attains immortality ' (in the passage under contemplation) means relative immortality and not absolute immortality. If the word Vidya in those texts meant the knowledge of the Paramatman, then the entreaty to the Sun for allowing a passage would become inappropriate. We therefore conclude with observing that our interpretation, *i. e.*, that the combination desired is of Karma with the worship of the deities and not with the Knowledge of the Paramatman is the purport of the mantras as commented upon by us.

Here ends the Commentary of Sankara Bhagavatpada on the Vajasaneya Samhitopanishad or Isavasyopanishad.

Om ! Peace ! Peace !! Peace !!!

Kenopanishad

Sri Sankara's Introduction.

ADORATION TO THE BRAHMAN.

OM TAT SAT.

This ninth chapter is begun for the purpose of publishing the Upanishad beginning with Keneshitam, etc.' and, treating of the Brahman. Before the beginning of the ninth chapter, all Karma has been explained and the different forms of worshipping Prâna, the source of all activity, have been laid down and all about the *Sâmans* (songs) preliminary to the rituals have been given. Next the *Gâyatra Sâman* has been explained and the genealogical list of preceptors and disciples has been given. All this Karma and Knowledge (of the deities) properly observed, as enjoined, tend to purify the mind of one who being free from desires, longs for emancipation. In the case of one who cherishes desires and has no knowledge, Karma by itself as laid down by the Srutis and the Smritis secures for him the southern route and return to Samsara. Activity following natural impulses and repugnant to the Sastras entails degradation into low births from beasts down to immovables. The Sruti says: "Travelling by neither of these two paths, these small creatures are constantly returning, of whom it may be said: 'Be born and die.' This is the third course." Another Sruti says "The three kinds of living beings (going by neither of these two paths) reach this miserable state." The desire to know the Brahman springs only in the person whose mind is pure, who is free from desires and who, free from deeds done in this birth or in previous ones, becomes disgusted with the external, ephemeral medley of ends and means. This Brahman is depicted in the Upanishad beginning with *Keneshitam*, etc., appearing in the form of questions and answers. Kâtaka says "The self-existent has made the senses external in their activity and man therefore looks outward, not at the self within." Some wise man having turned his eyes inward and being desirous of immortality saw the inner self. "Having examined the worlds reached by Karma let the Brâhmin grow disgusted (and learn to think that) nothing which is not made can be reached by Karma. In order to know that, let him, *Samidh* (sacrificial sticks) in hand, approach a preceptor who is well read in the Vedas and who is centred in Brahman". Thus in the Atharvanopanishad. In this way, and not otherwise, a man free from desires becomes qualified to hear, contemplate and acquire knowledge of the inner self. By the knowledge of the inner self, ignorance, which is the seed of bondage, and the cause of Karma performed for the realisation of desires, is entirely removed. The Srutis say: " There is no grief or delusion to one who sees this unity." " He who knows the Atman overcomes grief." " When He, that is both high and low, is seen, the knot of the heart is cut, all doubts are resolved and all Karma is consumed."

If it be urged that even by knowledge coupled with Karma this result is attained, we say no; for the Vâjasaneyaka shows that that combination produces different results. Beginning with " Let me have a wife," the texts go on to· say, " By a son should this world be gained, not by any other means; by Karma, the abode of the manes [Pitris]; and by knowledge, the world of the deities"; thus showing how the three worlds different from the Atman are reached. In the same place we find the following reason urged for·one becoming a Sanyasin : " What shall we, to whom this world is not the Atman, do with offspring?' The meaning is this: What shall we do with offspring, Karma, and Knowledge combined with Karma, which are the means to secure the world of the mortals the world of the manes, and the world of the Gods; and

which do not help us in securing the world of the
Atman? For, to us none of the three worlds, transitory and
attainable by these means, is desirable. To us that world
alone which is natural, unborn, undecaying, immortal,
fearless and neither augmented nor diminished by
Karma, and eternal, is covetable; and that being eternal
cannot be secured by any other means than the removal
of ignorance. Therefore the renunciation of all desires
preceded by the knowledge of the Brahman who is the
inner Self should alone be practised by us. Another reason is that the knowledge of the inner Self is
antagonistic to Karma and cannot therefore co-exist
with it. It is well known that the knowledge of the
Self, the one Atman of all, which abhors all perception
of difference cannot possibly co-exist with Karma whose
basis is the perception of the difference of agent, results,
etc. As knowledge relating to the reality, the knowledge of the Brahman is independent of human efforts.
Therefore the desire of a person, who is disgusted with
visible and invisible fruits achievable by external means,
to know the Brahman which is connected with the
inner Self, is indicated by the Sruti beginning with
Keneshitam, etc. The elucidation of the Brahman in
the form of a dialogue between the preceptor and the
disciple is, considering the subtle nature of the theme,
for the easy understanding thereof. It will also be

clearly pointed out that this knowledge is not to be attained solely by logical discussion. The Srutis say " This state of mind cannot be obtained by logical discussion." " He knows who has studied under a preceptor." " Such knowledge only as is acquired by studying under a preceptor does good." The Smriti lays down also " Learn That by prostration." It should be inferred that some one duly approached a preceptor centred in Brahman and finding no refuge except in his inner Self and longing for that which is fearless, eternal, calm and unshakable, questioned the preceptor as expressed in 'Keneshitam, etc.'

ALL-HAIL TO THE BRAHMAN.

Om Tat Sat.

सहनाववतु सह नौ भुनक्तु सह वीर्यं करवावहै ।
तेजस्विनावधीतमस्तु माविद्विषावहै ॥
ओं शान्तिः । शान्तिः । शान्तिः ।

May (Brahman) protect us both. May (Brahman) enjoy us both. May we work together. May the self-luminous Brahman be studied by us. May we not hate each other.

Om Peace ! Peace !! Peace !!!

आप्यायन्तु ममाङ्गानि वाक्प्राणश्चक्षुः श्रोत्रमथो बलमिन्द्रियाणि
च सर्वाणि सर्वं ब्रह्मौपनिषदं माहं ब्रह्म निराकुर्यां मा मा ब्रह्म नि-
राकारोदनिराकारणमस्त्वनिराकरणं मेऽस्तु तदात्मनि निरते य उप-
निषत्सु धर्मास्ते मयि सन्तु ते·मयि सन्तु ॥

ॐ शान्तिः । शान्तिः । शान्तिः ।

May my limbs, speech, *prâna*, eye, ear, strength and all my senses grow vigorous. All (everything) is the Brahman of the Upanishads. May I never deny the Brahman. May the Brahman never spurn me. May there be no denial of the Brahman. May there be no spurning by the Brahman. Let all the virtues recited by the Upanishads repose in me delighting in the Atman; may they in me repose.

Om Peace! Peace!! Peace!!!

केनेषितं पतति प्रेषितं मनः । केन प्राणः प्रथमः प्रैति युक्तः ।
केनेषितां वाचमिमां वदन्ति चक्षुः श्रोत्रं क उ देवो युनक्ति ॥

By whom willed and directed does the mind light on its subjects? By whom commanded does *prâna*, the first, move? By whose will do men speak this speech? What Intelligence directs the eye and the ear?

Commentary.—'*Kena*,' 'by what agent,' '*Ishitam*,' 'desired or directed.' '*Patati*,' 'goes' i.e., 'goes towards its ob-

jects.' As the root *Ish* cannot be here taken in the sense
of 'repeat' or 'go,' it must be understood to be used in
the sense of 'wish.' 'The *It* suffix in *Ishitam* is a case
of Vedic license. The word *Preshitam* is derived from
the same root, with *pra* before it, when it means 'direct.'
If the word *Preshitam* were alone used without the
word *Ishitam*, questions as to the nature of the director
and direction might arise, such as, by what sort of a
director and by what sort of direction. But the use
of the word *Ishitam* sets these two questions at rest,
for then the meaning clearly is: "By whose mere wish
is it directed, etc." It may be objected, that if this meaning were what was intended to be conveyed, the use of
the word *Preshitam* is rendered superfluous, as the
meaning intended is conveyed by *Ishitam* alone. It may
be also objected that as the use of more words should
convey more meaning, it is only reasonable to interpret
the text as meaning 'By what is it directed, by mere
will, by act or by word?' Both these objections are
unsound. From the mere fact of the question having
been asked, it is apparent that the question is asked by
one who is disgusted with the ephemeral conglomera-
tion of causes and effects, such as the body etc., and
who seeks to know something other than that—something unchangeable and eternal. Were it otherwise,
the question itself, seeing how notorious in the world

is the fact that the body directs by means of will,
act or word, would be meaningless. If it be objected that even on this view there is nothing gained in
the sense, by the use of the word *Preshitam*, we say
no. The word *Preshitam* adds to the sense when we
think that a questioner really entertains a doubt. To
show that the question is prompted by a doubt in the
questioner's mind, as to whether as is notorious, the
body—the collection of causes and effects—directs
the mind etc., or whether the mind etc. is directed by
the mere will of anything other than these combina-
tions of causes and effects and acting independently,
the use of both the words *Ishitam* and *Preshitam* is
justifiable. If, however, it be urged that the mind itself, as every body knows, independently lights on its
own object, and that the question is itself irrelevant,
the argument is untenable. If the mind were independent in the pursuit of its objects or in desisting from
pursuit, then it is not possible for any one to contemplate evil; but man, conscious of evil results, wills evil,
and the mind though dissuaded, attempts deeds of
serious evil consequences. Therefore the question
Kenoshitam etc. is certainly appropriate.

By whom directed does *Prâna* go, i.e., about its
own business? *Prathama* is an appropriate adjective of
Prâna, as the activity of all the sensory organs pre-

supposes it. By whom prompted is the speech which men in the world make use of? And what Intelligence directs the eye and the ear towards their respective objects?

श्रोत्रस्य श्रोत्रं मनसो मनो यद्वाचो ह वाचं स उ प्राणस्य प्राण-

धश्रुपधश्रुः ।

अतिमुच्य धीराः प्रेत्यास्माहोकादमृता भवंति ॥ २ ॥

2. It is the ear of the ear, mind of the mind, tongue of the tongue, and also life of the life and eye of the eye. Being disabused of the false notion, the wise, having left this body, become immortal.

Commentary.—To the worthy (disciple) who had thus questioned him, the preceptor in reply says: "Hear what you ask for—what intelligent Being directs the mind and the other senses towards their respective objects, and how it directs them." Ear is that by which one hears *i. e.*, the sense whose function is to hear sounds and distinguish them. He you asked for is the ear of that.

May it not be objected that while the reply ought to run in the form, 'So-and-so, with such-and-such attributes, directs the ear etc.' the reply in the form 'He is the ear of the ear etc.' is inappropriate? This is no objection; for he (the director) cannot otherwise be particularized. If the director of the ear etc., can be known by any activity of his own, independent of the activity of the ear etc., as a person who directs another to give, then indeed would this form of answer become inappropriate. But we do not here understand a director of the ear etc. having any activity of his own, like a mower. The director is inferred by logical necessity from the activity manifested by the ear and others combined, such as deliberation, volition, determination, enuring for the benefit of something distinct from them all (the ear etc). As things combined necessarily exist for the use of some other thing not so combined, we argue that there is a director of the ear etc., distinct from the ear etc., and for whose use the whole lot—the ear etc.,—exists in the same manner as a house exists for somebody's use. Hence the reply ' It is the ear of the ear etc.', is certainly appropriate.

Again it is asked what is the meaning of the expression : "It is the ear of the ear etc." And it is said that one ear does not want another, just as one light needs not another. This objection has no force. The meaning here is this. The ear has been found capable of perceiving objects and this capability of the ear depends upon the intelligence of the Atman, bright, eternal, intact, all-pervading. Therefore the expression ' It is the ear of the ear etc.' is correct. To the same effect also, the Srutis say, " He shines by his own bright-

ness." " By his light is all this Universe illumined."
" By that light illumined does the sun shine, etc." and
so on. The Bhagavad Gita says " As the light in the
sun illumines the whole world, so does the Atman
(Kshetri) O Bhârata! illumine all the body (Kshetrum)."
The Katha also says, "He is the eternal among the non-
eternal and the intelligence among the intelligent." The
' ear etc.' have been by all confounded with the Atman
and this false notion is here dispelled. The reply of
the preceptor : there is something indescribable, cognisable only by the intelligence of the wise, occupying
the deepest interior of all, unchangeable, undecaying,
immortal, fearless, unborn and ' the ear of the ear etc.'—
the source of all their functional capacity, is appropriate
and the meaning also. Similarly it is the mind of the
mind. It is evident that the mind, if not illumined by
the bright intelligence within, will be incapable of
performing its functions of volition, determination, etc.
It is therefore said that it is the mind of the mind.
Both the conditioned intelligence and mind are together contemplated by the word ' mind' in the text.
The word *yat* in ' *Yadvâchôharâcham*' means ' because' and should be read along with the words *Srôtra*
(ear), *manah* (mind) etc., thus : ' because it is the ear
of the ear', ' because it is the mind of the mind ' etc.
The objective case (*vâcham*) in ' *Vâchôharâcham*

should be converted into the nominative case; for we next read '*Pránasyapránah*.' It may be said that conformably to the expression '*Váchácharácham*' the following '*Pránasyapránah*' may as well be read as '*Pránasyapránam*.' It cannot be, for conformity to the majority is desirable. So '*vacham*' should be read as '*Vák*' in conformity to '*Sah*' and '*Pránah*' in '*Sa u pránasya pránah*,' because it then conforms with two words and conformity to the majority is preferred. Besides, the substance asked about can be best denoted by a noun in the nominative case. The substance asked about by you is the *prána of prána*, i.e., it is that substance which endows *prana* with the capacity to discharge its functions, i.e. to infuse activity; for there can possibly be no activity where the Atman does not preside. "Who could live and breatho if there were not the self-luminous Brahman;" and "Ho leads *Prana* up and *Apana* down" say the Sruties. It will also be said in this Upanishad, "You know That to be the Brahman which infuses activity into Prâna." It may be said that in a context speaking of the ear and other senses the mention of Breath would be more appropriate than that of Prâna. Truly so; but in the use of the word *prana*, breath is meant to be included.

The Sruti thinks thus:—the gist of this portion is that that is Brahman for whose use the aggregation of the

senses exerts its combined activity. Similarly it is the
oye of tho eye, &c. The capacity of tho eye to perceive
form is found only where the intelligenco of tho Atman
directs it. Therefore it is the eye of the eye. After
this expression in the text, the expression 'having understood the Brahman as abovo defined, i. e., as tho ear
of the ear &c.,' must be supplied by tho reader, as the
questioner should be supposed to be anxious to know
what ho asked about. Another reason why the expression should be supplied is tho enunciation of the result
'they become immortal;' for it is only by wisdom that
immortality is attained and it is only by knowledge one
can attain emancipation. *Having given up all the sensory organs*; (It is by confounding tho ear and other
sensory organs with the Atman that man is born subject
to these conditions, dies and thus rotates) means 'having
learnt that the Atman is the Brahman defined as the ear
of the ear &c.' *Atimuchya* means 'having given up tho
false notion that the ear, &c. is tho Atman'; for, without the aid of tho highest intelligence, it is impossible
for one to give up tho notion that the ear, &c., is
the Atman. '*Pretya*' means 'having turned away.'
'*Asmāllōkāt*' means 'from this world, where the talk
is always of 'my son,' 'my wife,' 'my kith and
kin.' Tho drift is 'having renounced all desires.'
'Become immortal' means 'enjoy immunity from

death.' The Srutis also say "Not by deeds, not by
offspring, not by wealth, but by renunciation did some
attain immortality"; "The senses were made to perceive only external objects;" "Having turned his senses
inwards for desire of immortality;" "When all desires
are driven forth, here they attain the Brahman" &c.
Or, seeing that the word *Atimuchya* necessarily implies
'renunciation of all desires,' the expression '*Asmâllôkâi
pretya*' may be interpreted as 'having left this mortal
body.'

न तत्र चक्षुर्गच्छति न वाग्गच्छति नो मनो न विद्मो न विजानीमो
यथैतदनुशिष्ट्याद्न्यदेव तद्विदितादधो अविदितादधि ।
इति शुश्रुम पूर्वेषां ये नस्तद्व्याचचक्षिरे ॥ ३ ॥

3. The eye does not go there, nor speech, nor mind.
We do not know That. We do not know how to instruct one about It. It is distinct from the known and
above the unknown. We have heard it so stated by
preceptors who taught us that.

Com.—For the reason that the Brahman is the ear
of the ear, *i. e.*, the Atman of all, the eye cannot go to
the Brahman ; for it is not possible to go to one's own
self. Similarly speech does not go there. When a word
spoken by the mouth enlightens the object denoted by
it, then the word is said to go to that object. But the

Atman of that word and of the organ that utters it is the
Brahman. So the word does not go there. Just as fire that
burns and enlightens things does not either enlighten
or burn itself, so the mind, which wills and determines
in respect of external objects, cannot will or determine
in respect of its self, because its Atman is also the Brahman. A thing is cognised by the senses and the mind.
We do not therefore know the Brahman, because it
cannot be an object of perception to these ; and we do
not therefore know what the Brahman is like, so as to
allow us to enlighten the disciple about the Brahman.
Whatever can be perceived by the senses, it is possible
to explain to others by epithets denoting its class, its
attributes and modes of activity ; but the Brahman has
no attributes of class, etc.   It therefore follows that it
is not possible to make the disciple believe in the Brahman by instruction.   The portion of the text beginning with ' *Navidmah* ' (we do not know) shows the
necessity of putting forth great exertion in the matter
of giving instruction and understanding it, in respect
of the Brahman. Considering that the previous portion of the text leads to the conclusion that it is impossible by any means to instruct one about the Atman, the following exceptional mode is pointed out.
Indeed it is true that one cannot be persuaded to believe in the Brahman by the evidence of the senses and

other modes of proof; bnt it is possible to make him
believe by the aid of *Agamas* (Scriptures). Therefore
the preceptor recites *Agamas* for the purposo of teaching about the Brahman and says: 'It is something distinct from the known and something beyond the unknown, etc.' '*Anyat*,' 'something distinct'; 'Tat,' 'tho
present theme'; i.e., that which has been defined to bo
the car of the ear, etc., and beyond their (ear, eye, etc.,)
reach. That is certainly distinct from the known. 'The
known,' means 'whatever is the object of special knowledge'; and as all such objects can be known somewhere,
to some extent and by some one and so forth, the whole
(manifested universe) is meant by tho term 'the
known'; the drift is, that the Brahman is distinct from
this. But lest the Brahman should be confounded with
the unknown, the text says: 'It is beyond the Unknown.'
'*Aviditât*' means 'something opposed to the known;'
hence, unmanifested illusion (avidya) the seed of all
manifestation. '*Adhi*' literally means 'above' but is hero
used in the derivativo sense of 'something different from';
for, it is well known that one thing placed abovo
another is something distinct from that other.

Whatever is known is little, mortal and full of misery
and therefore fit to be abandoned. Therefore when it
is said that Brahman is distinct from the Known
it is clear that it is not to be abandoned. Simi-

larly, when the Brahman is said to be distinct from
the Unknown it is in effect said that the Brahman is not
fit to be taken. It is to produce an effect that one seeks
for a cause. Therefore there can be nothing distinct
from the knower, which the knower could seek for, with
any benefit. Thus, by saying that the Brahman is distinct from both the Known and the Unknown and thus
disproving its fitness to be abandoned or to be taken, the
desire of the disciple to know anything distinct from Self
(Atman) is checked. For, it is clear that none other than
one's Atman can be distinct from both the Known and
the Unknown ; the purport of the text is that the Atman
is Brahman. The Srutis also say : "This Atman is
Brahman"; "this Atman who is untouched by sin".
"This is the known and the unkown Brahman;" "This
Atman is within all ;" etc. The preceptor next says how
this meaning of the text, that the Atman of all, marked by no distinguishing attributes, bright and intelligent, is the Brahman, has been traditionally handed
down from preceptor to disciple. And Brahman can be
known only by instruction from preceptors and not by
logical disquisitions, nor by expositions, intelligence,
great learning, penance or sacrifices etc. We have heard
this saying 'of. the preceptors who clearly taught us
the Brahman.

यद्वाचानभ्युदितं येन वागभ्युद्यते ।
तदेव ब्रह्म त्वं विद्धि नेदं यदिदमुपासते ॥ ४ ॥

4. What speech does not enlighten, but what enlightens speech, know that alone to be the Brahman,
not this which (people) here worship.

Com.—When by the text "It is something distinct
from both the known and the unknown," the preceptor
conveyed that the Atman is Brahman, the disciple
doubted how the Atman could be Brahman. The Atman,
as is well known, being entitled to perform *karma*
and worship (of the gods) and being subject to births
and re-births seeks to attain Brahma or other Devas, or
heaven, by means of Karma or worship. Therefore,
somebody other than the Atman, such as Vishnu,
Iswara, Indra or Prâna, entitled to be worshipped,
may well be Brahman; but the Atman can never be; for,
it is contrary to popular belief. Just as logicians contend that the Atman is distinct from Iswara, so the vo-
taries of Karma worship Devas, other than the Atman,
saying : 'Propitiate this Deva by sacrifice' and 'Propitiate that Deva by sacrifice.' Therefore it is only
reasonable that what is known and entitled to worship
is Brahman and that the worshiper is other than that.
The preceptor inferred this doubt running in the disciple's mind either from his looks or from his words

and said : 'Do not doubt thus.' *Yat* means 'that which is intelligence itself." *Vâk* is the organ presided over by Agni (Fire) occupying eight localities in the body, such as the root of the tongue, &c. The letters are intended to express the meaning to be conveyed and are subject to laws as to their number and order. The word which is produced by them is called *Vâk* (speech). The Sruti says "The letter *a* is all speech, which being produced by the use of letters, divided into *sparsa, an-tastha* and *ushma* becomes divorse and assumes many forms." The Rik, Yajur, Sama and truth and falsehood are its modifications. By such speech enclosed in words and conditioned by the organ of speech, Brahman is not illumined or explained. '*Yena*', 'by the Brahman.' Brahman by its brightness illumines speech and its organ. It has been said here that, That (Brahman) is the speech of speech. The Vâjasaneyaka says ' Brahman is within the speech and directs it.' Having said 'Speech in man is the same as that in the letters and that some Brâhmin knows it,' the Upanishad, in answer to a question anticipated, says "That is speech, by which one speaks in dreams." The speaker's power of speech is eternal, and is by nature of the same essence as Intelligence. The power of speech of the speaker knows no decay. So says the Sruti. Know this Atman to be the Brahman, unsurpassable, known as Bhû-

ma. *Brahman*, because it is big, all-pervading ; know
this through its conditions of speech, etc. The following expressions 'speech of speech,' 'eye of the eye,' 'ear
of the ear,' 'mind of the mind,' 'doer,' 'enjoyer,' 'know-
or,' 'controllor,' 'governor,' 'Brahman is knowledge and
bliss,' etc., are used in popular language of the un-
speakable Brahman, devoid of attributes, highest of all,
unchangeable. Disregarding these, know the Atman
itself to be the unconditioned Brahman. This is the
meaning. Brahman is not what people here worship,
such as Iswara, which is not the Atman, and which is
conditioned and referred to as 'this'. Though it had
been said: 'know That to be Brahman'; still it is again
said : "and not this, etc." thus repeating the idea that,
what is not Atman is not Brahman. This is either to
lay down a *Niyama* (a rule restricting the choice to a
stated alternative when several others are possible) or
for *Parisankhyâna* (exclusion.)

यन्मनसा न मनुते येनाहुर्मनो मतम् ।
तदेव ब्रह्म त्वं विद्धि नेदं यदिदमुपासते ॥ ५ ॥

5· What one can think with the mind, but by
which they say the mind is thought out, know That
alone to be the Brahman, not this which (people) here
worship.

Com.—'*Manah*,' 'mind.' By the word '*Manah*' here, both mind and intelligence are meant. ' *Manah*' means 'that by which one thinks.' The mind is equally connected with all the sensory organs, because its sphere includes all external objects. The Sruti says : ' Desire, volition, deliberation, faith, negligence, boldness, timidity, shame, intelligence, fear, all those are mind.' The modes of activity of the mind are desire, etc. By that mind, none wills or determines that intelligence which enlightens the mind, because as enlightener of the mind, that is the mind's controller, the Atman being in the interior of everything, the mind cannot go there. The capacity of the mind to think exists, because it is enlightened by the intelligence shining within, and it is by that, that the mind is capable of activity. Those who know the Brahman say that the mind is pervaded by the Brahman. Therefore know that to be the Brahman which is the Atman, the interior intelligence of the mind. ' *Nadam*, etc.,' has already been explained in the commentary on the last verse.

यच्चक्षुषा न पश्यति येन चक्षूंषि पश्यति ।

तदेव ब्रह्म त्वं विद्धि नेदं यदिदमुपासते ॥ ६ ॥

7

6. What none sees by the eye, but by which seeing is seen, That alone know thou to be the Brahman; not this which (people) here worship.

Com.—'See' means 'perceive as an object.' By the light of the Atman, connected with the activities of the mind, man perceives the activity of tho eye, varying with the activity of the mind.

यच्छ्रोत्रेण न शृणोति येन श्रोत्रमिद्ँश्रुतम् ।

तदेव ब्रह्म त्वं विद्धि नेदं यदिदमुपासते ॥ ७ ॥

7. What none hears with the ear, but by which hearing is heard, That alone know thou to be tho Brahman; not this which (people) here worship.

Com.—'What none hears with the ear' means 'what the world does not perceive as an object with the organ of hearing, presided over by *Digdevata*, produced in Akas and connected with the activity of the mind.' 'By which this hearing is heard,' it is well known that it is perceived as an object by the intelligence of the Atman. The rest has been already explained.

यत्प्राणेन न प्राणिति येन प्राणः प्रणीयते ।

तदेव ब्रह्म त्वं विद्धि नेदं यदिदमुपासते ॥ ८ ॥

8. What none breathes with the breath, but by which breath is in-breathed, That alone know thou to be the Brahman; not this which (people) here worship.

Com.—' What none breathes with the breath' means ' what none perceives, like odour, with the earthly breath filling the nostrils and connected with the activity of the mind and life.' ' But by which, etc.' means ' by the enlightening intelligence of the Atman, breath is made to move towards its objects.' All the rest ' *tadeva*, etc.' has already been explained.

Here ends the first part.

———0———

Kenopanishad.

SECOND PART

यदि मन्यसे सुवेदेति दहरमेवापि नूनम् ।
त्वं वेत्थ ब्रह्मणो रूपं यदस्य त्वं यदस्य देवेष्वथ नु मीमा ५स्य-
मेव ते मन्ये विदितम् ॥ ९ ॥

1.   If thou thinkest 'I know well' it is certainly but
little—the form of the Brahman thou hast known, as
also the form in the Devas. Therefore I think that
what thou thinkest known is still to be ascertained.

Com.—The preceptor, fearing that the disciple, persuaded to believe that he is the Atman *i.e.*, the Brahman
not fit to be abandoned or acquired, might think 'I certainly am the Brahman, I know myself well,' says for the
purpose of dispelling that notion of the disciple '*Yadi*
etc'. Then, is not an accurate conviction 'I know (Brahman) well' desirable?. Certainly it is desirable. But an
accurate conviction is not of the form 'I know (Brahman) well'. If what should be known becomes an ob-

ject of sense-perception then it is possible to know it well, just as an inflammable substance can be consumed by the consuming fire. But the essence of fire cannot itself be so consumed. The well-ascertained drift of all Vedanta is that the self (Atman) of every knower is the Brahman. The same has been here explained in the form of question and answer by the text 'It is the ear of the ear etc'. The same has been still more clearly determined by the text: "What is not enlightened by speech, etc". The traditional theory of those who know the Brahman has also been declared by the text: "It is something different from both the known and the unknown". This Upanishad will also conclude by saying "It is unknown to those who know, and known to those who do not know". It is therefore certainly proper that the notion of the disciple, 'I know, Brahman well' should be dispelled. It is evident that the knower cannot be known by the knower, just as fire cannot be consumed by fire. There is no knower other than the Brahman, to whom the Brahman can be a knowable, distinct from himself. By the Sruti: "There is no knower other than that," the existence of another knower is denied. The belief therefore 'I know Brahman well' is an illusion. Therefore well did the preceptor say 'Yadi, etc'. 'Yadi' means 'if perchance'. 'Suveda' means 'I know Brahman well'. Because some one whose

sins have been purged and who is really intelligent
may properly understand what is taught and others
not, the preceptor begins with a doubt 'Yadi' etc'. Such
cases have also been found to occur. When he was in-
formed 'This *purusha* who is seen in the eye, this is
the Atman; this is the immortal, fearless self,' Viró-
chana, the son of Prajâpati and the lord of the Asuras,
though intelligent, misinterpreted this instruction on
account of his natural defects and understood that the
body was the Atman. Similarly, Indra, lord of the Devas, not being able to comprehend the Brahman, at the
first, second and third instructions, did, at the fourth,
his natural faults having been removed, comprehend
the very Brahman that he was first taught. It has been
found in the world also, that, of disciples receiving instruction from the same preceptor, some understand him
properly, some misinterpret his teaching, some interpret it into the exact contrary of the teacher's view and
some do not understand it at all. What more need we
say of the knowledge of the Atman which is beyond
the reach of the senses. On this point, all logicians,
with their theories of *Sat* and *Asat*, are in conflict. The
doubt therefore expressed in 'Yadi *manyase*' etc., with
which the preceptor begins his discourse is certainly
appropriate, considering that the disciples, in spite of
the instruction that the Brahman is unknowable, might

have misunderstood him. '*Dahara*' means 'little'; '*Vettha*' means 'knowest'; *i.e.*, thou knowest surely littlo of Brahman's form. Has Brahman then many forms, great and little, that it is said '*daharam* etc.'? Quite so; many indeed are the forms of Brahman produced by conditions of name and form, but none in reality. By nature, as the Sruti says, it is without sound, touch, form, destruction; likewise tasteless, odourless, and eternal. Thus with sound, etc., form is denied. But it may be said that, as that by which a thing is defined, is its *rúpa* or form, tho peculiar atttibuto of Brahman by which it is defined, may bo said to bo its form. Wo thus answer. Intelligence cannot bo the quality of tho earth, etc., either of one or all of them together, or under any modifications. Similarly, it cannot be the quality of the sensory organs, like the ear, etc., or of the mind. '*Brahmano rúpam*', Brahman is defined by its intelligence. Henco it is said : "Brahman is knowledge and bliss'; 'Brahman is denso with knowlodge '; 'Brahman is existence, knowledge and infinity '; thus the form of Brahman has been defined. Truly so ; but even there, the Brahman is defined by tho words 'knowledge, etc'., only with reference to the limitations of mind, body and senses, because of its apparent adaptations to the expansion, contraction, extinction etc., of tho body etc., and not on account of its own essence. According

to its essence it will be concluded in the subsequent
portion of this Upanishad that it is unknown to those
who know, and known to those who do not know. The
expression ' *Yadasya brahmano rúpam* ' should be read
along with what precedes it. Not only dost thou
know little of the form of Brahman, when thou knowest
it as conditioned in man, but also when thou knowest
it as conditioned in the Devas ; so I think. Even the
form of Brahman as it exists in the Devas is little, because it is limited by condition. The gist is that the
Brahman limited by no conditions or attributes, passive,
infinite, one without a second, known as Bhúma, eternal,
cannot be known well. This being so, I think that
you have yet to know Brahman by enquiry. ' *Atha nu*,'
' therefore.' ' *Mimâmsyam*,' ' worthy of enquiry.' Thus
addressed by the preceptor, the disciple sat in solitude
all composed, discussed within himself the meaning of
the Agama as pointed out by his Guru (preceptor),
arrived at a conclusion by his reasoning, realised it in
himself, approached the preceptor and exclaimed " I
think I now know Brahman."

नाहं मन्ये सुवेदेति नो न वेदेति वेद च ।
यो नस्तद्वेद तद्वेद नो न वेदेति वेद च ॥ १० ॥

I do not think I know well; I know too; not that I
do not know. He of us who knows that, knows that

8

as also what is meant by 'I know too; not that I do not know.'

Com.—On being asked how, the disciple says: "Listen. I do not think I know Brahman well." "Then is the Brahman not known by theo?" Thus questioned, the disciple says "Not that I do not know, I know too;" the word *too* in 'I know too' means 'I do not know too'. Is it not contradictory: 'I think I know not Brahman well etc'? If thou dost not think thou knowest well, how then dost thou think thou knowest also? If again thou think-est thou certainly knowest, then how dost thou think thou knowest not well? To say that a thing is not known well by the man who knows it is a contradiction, tho cases of doubt and false knowledge being left out of consideration. Nor is it possible to lay down a restrict-ive rule that the knowledge of Brahman should bo doubtful or false. It is well known that under any cir-cumstances, doubtful or false knowledge works great evil. Though thus attempted to bo shaken in his con-viction by the preceptor the disciple was not shaken. From the tradition which his master had explained to him, *i.o.*, that tho self is something other than both the known and tho unknown, from the reasonableness of the doctrino and from tho strength of his own experience the disciple loudly exclaimed, showing the firmness of his knowledge of the Brahman. How ho exclaimed is thus stated. 'He of us,' i.e., my co-disciple, who correctly understands what I have said knows That (Brahman). The words he referred to are 'not that I do not know. I know too'. What was defined by the expression 'that is something other than both the known and the unknown', the disciple discussed and decided from inference and from experience; and in order to see whether the preceptor's views agreed with his own and to counteract any false conclusion, which dull persons may have arrived at, he expressed the same in different words : 'not that I do not know; I know too'. The confident exclamation of the disciple 'He of us, etc.,' is accordingly appropriate.

यस्यामतं तस्य मतं मतं यस्य न वेद सः ।

अविज्ञातं विजानतां विज्ञातमविजानतां ॥ ३ ॥

3. It is Known to him to whom it is Unknown; he knows it not to whom it is Known. (It is) Unknown to those who know, and Known to those who do not know.

Com.—Turning from the concurring views of the preceptor and the disciple, the Sruti speaking for itself conveys in this text the view about which there is no disagreement. The purport is that to the knower of the Brahman whose firm conviction is that the Brahman is unknowable, the Brahman is well known. But he,

whoso conviction is that tho Brahman is known by him,
certainly knows not the Brahman. The latter half of
tho text, only states those two distinct conclusions of
tho wiso and ignorant man more emphatically. To those
who know well, the Brahman is certainly (a thing) unknown; but to those who do not see well, i.e., who con-
found tho Atman with the sensory organs, the mind and
the conditioned intelligence [Buddhi], Brahman is certainly not known, but not to those who aro extremely ignorant ; for, in the case of these, the thought 'Brahman
is known by us' never arises. In the case of those who
find the Atman in the conditioned organs of sense,
mind and intelligence, the false notion ' I know Brahman ' is quite possible, because they cannot discriminate
between Brahman and these conditions and because
the conditions of intelligence etc. are known to them.
It is to show that such knowledge of the Brahman is
fallacious that the latter half of tho text is introduced.
Or, the latter half ' Avignâtum, etc.', may be construed
as furnishing a reason for tho view propounded in tho
former.

प्रतिबोधविदितं मतममृतत्वं हि विन्दते ।

आत्मना बिन्दते वीर्यं विद्यया बिन्दतेऽमृतं ॥ १२ ॥

4. (The Brahman) is known well, when it is known
as the witness of every state of consciousness ; for (by

such knowledge) one attains immortality. By his self
he attains strength and by knowledge, immortality.

Com.—It has been settled that it is unknown to those
who know. If Brahman be not known at all, it will then
come to this, that there is no difference between the
worldly-minded and those who know the Brahman. To
say that It is unknown to those who know is also a contradiction. How then could that Brahman be well-known?
This is explained in this text. *'PratiVôdhavidilum'*
means 'known in respect of every state of consciousness.'
By the word 'bodha' is meant 'mental perception'. That
by which all states of consciousness are perceived like
objects is the Atman. He knows and sees all states of
consciousness, being by nature nothing but intelligence
and is indicated by these states of consciousness, as
blended with every one of them. There is no other
way by which the inner Atman could be known.
Therefore when the Brahman is known as the witness
of all states of consciousness, then it is known well.
Being the witness of all states of consciousness, it will
be clear that it is intelligence in its essence, subject
to neither birth nor death, eternal, pure, unconditioned,
and one in all things, because there is no difference in its
essence, just as in the essence of the *Akás*, in a vessel or
mountain cave, etc. The drift of the passage from the
Agamas [traditions] is that the Brahman is other than

both the known and the unknown. It is this pure Atman that will be described at the close of the Upanishad. Another Sruti says "He is the seer of the eye, the hearer of the ear, the thinker of thought, and the knower of knowledge." But some explain the expression ' *Pratibôdhaviditam* ' in the text as meaning 'known by its defining attribute of knowledge,' on the view that Brahman is the author of the act of knowing and that Brahman as such author is known by its activity in knowing,' just as the wind is known as that which shakes the branches of the trees. In this view the Atman is an unintelligent substance having the power to know and not intelligence itself. Consciousness is produced and is destroyed. When consciousness is produced, then the Atman is associated with it ; but when it is destroyed, the Atman, dissociated from consciousness, becomes a mere unintelligent substance. Such being the case, it is not possible to get over the objection that the Atman is rendered changeable in its nature, composed of parts, transient, impure, etc. Again according to the followers of Kanâda consciousness is said to be produced by the combination of the Atman and the mind and to adhere to the Atman. Therefore the Atman possesses the attribute of knowledge but is not subject to modifications. It simply becomes a substance just like a pot made red. Even on this theory the Brahman is reduced to an unintelligent substance and therefore the Srutis ' Brahman is knowledge and bliss, etc.' would be set at naught. Moreover the Atman having no parts and being omnipresent and therefore over connected (with the mind), the impossibility of laying down a law regulating the origin of recollection is an insurmountable objection.

Again that the Atman can be connected with any thing is itself repugnant to the Srutis, Smritis and logic. 'The Atman is not connected with anything else'; 'The Atman unconnected with anything supports everything'; so say both the Sruti and the Smriti. According to logic too, a thing having attributes may be connected with another having attributes and not with one dissimilar in class. To say therefore, that a thing having no attribute, undifferentiated and having nothing in common with anything else combines with another unequal in class is illogical. Therefore the meaning that the Atman is, by nature, knowledge and light, eternal and undecaying, can be arrived at only if the Atman be the witness of all states of consciousness, and not otherwise. Hence the meaning of the expression ' *Pratibôdhaviditam matam* ' is just what we explained it to be. Some, however, explain that the drift of this portion of the text is that the Atman is knowable by itself. There the Atman is thought of as

conditioned and people talk of knowing the Atman by
the Atman, distinguishing as it were, the unconditioned
Atman from the Atman conditioned by intelligence,
etc.   Thus it has been said "He sees the Atman by
the Atman," and " O Best of men ! know the Atman
by the Atman, thyself." It is clear that the unconditioned Atman, being one, is not capable of being
known either by itself or by others.   Being itself the
knowing principle, it cannot stand in need of another
knowing principle ; just as one light cannot possibly require another light. So here. On the theory of the followers of Buddha that the Atman is known by itself, knowledge becomes momentary and no Atman as its knower
is possible. It is well known that the knowledge of the
knower knows no destruction, being indestructible.
Again the Srutis : "Him who is eternal omnipresent and
all-pervading", 'This is He, great, unborn, Atman, undecaying, deathless, immortal and fearless,' etc., would
be set at naught. Some, however, construe the word
' Pratibôdha ' to mean ' causeless perception ' as that of
one who sleeps. Others yet say that the word 'Pratibôdha' means 'knowledge of the moment'. (We answer)
whether it has or has not a cause, whether it occurs
once or is often repeated, it is still Pratibôdha itself or
knowledge itself. The drift is that the Brahman known
as the witness of all states of consciousness is well-

known, because by such knowledge, one attains immortality, i.e., being centred in one's self, i.e., emancipation. The knowledge that the Atman is the witness of all states of consciousness is the reason for immortality. Immortality cannot possibly be the fact of the Atman becoming something other than itself. The immortality of the Atman, consisting in being Atman, is causeless; thus the mortality of the Atman consists in the mistaken belief of 'no Atman' induced by ignorance. How again, it may be asked, does one attain immortality by the knowledge of the Atman as already explained? It is therefore said as follows: '*Atmana*' means 'by one's own nature'; '*Vindate*' means 'attains'; '*Viryam*' means 'strength or capacity.' The strength gained by wealth, retinue, mantras, medicinal herbs, devotion and *yoga* cannot overcome mortality, because that is produced by things themselves mortal. The strength gained by the knowledge of the Atman can be acquired by the Atman alone and not by any other means. Because the strength produced by the knowledge of the Atman does not require any other aid, that strength alone can overcome death. And because one acquires by his Atman alone the strength produced by the knowledge of the Atman, therefore he attains immortality by the knowledge of the Atman. The Atharvana Upanishad says "This Atman cannot be attained by one devoid of strength."

9

इह चेद्वेदादथ सत्यमस्ति न चेदिहावेदीन्महती विनष्टि: ।
भूतेषु भूतेषु विचिल्य धीरा: प्रेत्यास्माल्लोकादमृता भवन्ति ॥१३॥

5. If one knows (That) here, then there is truth.
If one knows not (That) here, there will be great loss.
The wise, seeing the one Atman in all created things,
having turned away from this world, become immortal.

Com :—It is indeed hard to suffer birth, old age,
death, sickness, etc. owing to ignorance, being one of
the crowd of living beings such as Devas, men, beasts,
(*pretas*), etc., full of the miseries of Samsara. Therefore
if a man, even in this world being authorised and competent, knows the Atman as defined, in the manner
already explained, then there is truth ; *i.e.*, there is
in this birth as a mortal, immortality, usefulness,
real existence. But if one living here and authorised
does not know the Brahman, then there is long
and great misery for him, *i.e.*, rotation in Samsara—
one continuous stream of births and deaths. Therefore
the Brâhmins who know the advantages and the dis-
advantages as above pointed out, perceive in all things
in the universe, immovable and movable, the one essence of the Atman *i.e.*, the Brahman, turn away with
disgust from this world, the creature of ignorance consisting in the false notion of 'I' and 'mine' and having
realised the principle of unity. the oneness of the At-

man in all, become immortal, *i.e.*, become Brahman itself; for the Sruti says "He who knows that highest Brahman becomes Brahman itself."

Here ends the Second Part.

———0———

Kenopanishad.

——o——

ब्रह्म ह देवेभ्यो विजिग्ये तस्य ह ब्रह्मणो विजये देवा अमह्वीयन्त ।
त ऐक्षन्तास्माकमेवायं विजयोऽस्माकमेवायं महिमेति ॥ १४ ॥

The Brahman won a victory for the Devas and in
that victory of the Brahman the Devas attained glory.
They thought 'the victory is ours and this glory is
ours alone'.

Com.—From the passage that 'It is not known to those
who know,' some fools may argue that whatever is, can
be known by proofs, and whatever is not cannot bo so
known and is therefore non-existent, as the horns of a
hare, and Brahman, being unknown, does not exist.
In order that they may not fall into that error this par-
able is introduced; for, the subsequent passages clearly
show the folly of thinking that that Brahman who is
controllor of all in every way, Deva, even superior to
all Devas, Lord over lords, not easily known, the cause
of the victory of the Devas and of the defeat of tho
Asuras, does not exist. Or (it is related) for eulogising

the knowledge of Brahman. How ? By showing that
it was indeed by the knowledge of the Brahman that
Fire, etc., attained pre-eminence among the Devas; and
Indra specially more than the rest. Or, it shows how
difficult it is to know Brahman, because even Fire. etc,
with all their great powers, and even Indra, lord of the
Devas knew the Brahman only with considerable diffi-
culty. It may be that the whole Upanishad to follow
is intended to lay down an injunction (to know the
Brahman) or the story may have been intended to show
the fallacious nature of the notion of doer, etc., found
in all living beings, by contrasting it with the knowledge of the Brahman—fallacious like the notion of the
Devas that the victory was theirs. The Brahman already
defined won a victory for the benefit of the Devas ; i.e.,
the Brahman in a battle between the Devas and the
Asuras defeated the Asuras, the enemies of the world
and the violaters of the limitations imposed by the
Lord and gave the benefit of the victory to the Devas
for the preservation of the world. In this victory of
Brahman the Devas, Fire, etc., attained glory, and not
knowing that the victory and glory belonged to the
Paramâtman, seated in their own Atman, the witness
of all perceptions, Lord of the universe, omniscient, the
dispenser of the fruits of all Karma, omnipotent,
and desirous of securing the safety of the world, looked

upon the victory and the glory, as achieved by themselves—the Atman enclosed within the limitations of
their own forms, Fire, etc. ; that the glory—their being
Fire, Air, Indra and the like, resulting from the victory
—was theirs and that neither the victory nor the glory
belonged to the Lord, over all the Atman within them.
So they cherished this false notion.

तद्धैषां विजज्ञौ तेभ्यो ह प्रादुर्बभूव तन्न व्यजानत किमिदं यक्षमिति
॥ १५ ॥

2.   He know this notion of theirs and appeared before them.   What that Great Spirit was   they did   not
know.

Com.—The Brahman evidently knew this false notion
of theirs. Brahman being omniscient and director of the
senses of all living beings knew of the false idea of the
Devas and in order that the Devas might not be dis-
graced like the Asuras by this false notion, out of pity
for them and intending to bless them by dispelling.
their false notion, appeared before them for their benefit in a form assumed at will, in virtue of its power—
a form unprecedentedly glorious and astonishing and
capable of being perceived by the senses. The Devas
did not at all know the Brahman that appeared before
them.   Who is this *Yaksham, i.e.,* this venerable Great
Spirit.

तेऽग्निमब्रुवन् जातवेद एतद्विजानीहि किमिदं यक्षमिति तथेति ॥ ३ ॥
तदभ्यद्रवत्तमभ्यवदत्कोऽसीत्यग्निर्वा अहमस्मी त्यब्रवीज्जातवेदा वा
अहमस्मीति ॥ ४ ॥ तस्मि ५स्त्वयि किं वीर्यमित्यपीद ५ सर्व दहेयं
यदिदं पृथिव्यामिति ॥ ५ ॥ तस्मै तृणं निदधावेतद्दहेति तदुपप्रेयाय
सर्वजवेन तन्न शशाक दग्धुं स तत एव निववृते नैतदशकं वि-
ज्ञातुं यदेतन्यक्षमिति ॥ ६ ॥

3. They addressed the Fire thus "O Játaveda! Find
out what this Great Spirit is." Ho said "yes."

4. He ran to That. That said to him "who art
thou"? He replied "I am Agni or I am Játaveda."

5. That said "what power, in thee so named, is
lodged." He replied "I can burn even all this, on the
earth."

6. That placed a straw before him and said : 'Burn
this.' He approached it with all haste but was not able
to burn it. He immediately returned from thence to
the Devas and said "I was not able to learn what this
Great Spirit is."

Com.—The Devas not knowing what that Spirit was,
being afraid of it, and desirous to know what it was, thus
addressed Agni who went before them and who was
little less than omniscient. "O Játaveda, learn well
what this Great Spirit now in our view is. You are

the brightest of us all." "Be it so" said Agni and ran towards the Spirit. Seeing him approach near, with a desire to ask questions of it, but overawed into silence in its presence, the Spirit asked him: "who art thou?". Thus questioned by Brahman, Agni replied: "I am Agni well known also as Jâtaveda"; as if in self-complaisance at being so well known by two names, Brahman said to Agni who had thus replied: "what power is in thee who ownest such well-known and significant names?." He replied: "I could reduce to ashes all this universe and all immoveables, etc., on this earth." The word 'earth' is illustratively used; for, even what is in the air is burnt by Agni [Fire]. The Brahman placed a straw before Agni who was so vain-glorious, and said: "Burn but this straw in my presence. If thou art not able to burn this, give up thy vanity as the consumer of all." Thus addressed, Agni approached the straw with all the spesd of over-ween-ing confidence but was not able to burn it. So he, Jâtaveda, being unable to burn it, covered with shame and baffled in his resolution, returned in silence from the presence of the Spirit and told the Devas: "I was not able to learn more, concerning this Spirit."

अथ वायुमब्रुवन् वायवेतद्विजानीहि किमेतद्यक्षमिति तथेति ॥७॥
तदभ्यद्रवत्तमभ्यवदत्कोऽसीति वायुर्वा अहमस्मीत्यब्रवीन्मातरिश्वा

वा अहमस्मीति ॥ ८ ॥ तस्मि ५स्त्वयि किं वीर्यमिलपींद ५सर्व-
माददीयं यदिदं पृथिव्यामिति ॥ ९ ॥ तस्मै तृणं निदधावेतदा-
दत्स्वेति तदुपप्रेयाय सर्वजवेन तन्न शशाकाऽऽदातुं स तत एव निव-
वृते नैतदशकं विज्ञातुं यदेतच्चक्षमिति ॥ १० ॥

7. The Devas then said to Air: "Learn O Vayu!
what this Great Spirit is" He said: "yes."
8. He ran to That. That said: "who art thou"?
He replied: "I am Air or Mâtarisva."
9. That said "what power is in thee; so well
known?" He replied: "I can blow away all the universe
and all that is on the earth."
10. That placed a straw before him and said "Blow
it away." He approached it with all speed but was not
able to blow it. He returned immediately from there
and told the Devas "I was not able to learn who this
Great Spirit is."

Com.—They next addressed Air thus: 'know this, etc.'
The rest bears the same meaning as in the last passage.
Vâyu [Air] is so named from the root which means 'to
go' or 'to smell'. Air is also called 'Mâtarisva' because
it travels [Svayuti] in space [Mâtari]. 'Adadiyam' means
'can take'. The rest is explained as in the previous
passage.

अथेन्द्रमब्रुवन्मववन्नेतद्द्विजानीहि किमेतद्यक्षामिति तथेति त-
दभ्यद्रवत्तस्मात्तिरोदधे ॥ ११ ॥ स तस्मिन्नेवाकाशे स्त्रियमाज-
गाम बहुशोभमानामुमा ×हैमवत तां ता ×होवाच किमेतद्यक्षामिति
॥ १२ ॥

11. Then they said to Indra : "O Maghavan! learn what this Great Spirit is." He said "yes " and ran to That. That vanished from his view.

12. Ho beheld in that very spot a woman, Uma, very beautiful and of golden hue, daughter of Himavat. He said to her " What is this Great Spirit".

Com.—Atha, etc., has already been explained. Indra, lord of the Devas, Maghavan, (being the most powerful of them) said yes, and ran to That. But That vanished from his sight, when he was near the Brahman and did not even talk to him, because it wished to crush altogether his pride at being Indra. In the very spot where the Spirit showed itself and from which it vanished and near the place where Indra was at the moment the Brahman vanished, Indra stood discussing within himself what that Spirit was, and did not return like Agni and Vayu. Seeing his attachment to that Spirit, knowledge in the form of a woman and of Uma appeared before him. Indra beheld knowledge, fairest of the fair,—this epithet is very appropriate in the particular context—as if adorned in gold. '*Himavatim*' may mean 'the daughter of Himâlaya', and being ever associated with the Lord (Siva) the omniscient, and having approached her, asked: "Who is this Spirit that showed itself and vanished ?"

Here ends the Third Part.

—o—

Kenopanishad.

FOURTH PART.

सा ब्रह्मेति होवाच ब्रह्मणोवा एतद्विजये महीयध्वमिति ततो हैव
विदाश्वकार ब्रह्मेति ॥ १ ॥

She said " It is Brahman indeed. Attain glory in
the victory of Brahman." From her words only, he
learned that it was Brahman.

Com.—The particle ' *Ha* ' means ' verily '. Glory in
the victory of the omnipotent Lord (for the Asuras
were defeated only by Brahman). *Etat* modifies the
predicate. Your notion that the victory and tho glory
are yours is false. From her words alone Indra learned
that it was Brahman. The force of 'only' is that Indra
did not know of himself.

तस्माद्वा एते देवा अतितरामिवान्यान्देवान्यदग्निर्वायुरिन्द्रस्ते
ह्येनन्नेदिष्ठं पस्पृशुस्ते ह्येनत्प्रथमो विदाश्वकार ब्रह्मेति ॥ २ ॥

2. These Devas, Agni, Vâyu and Indra therefore
much excel others, because they touchod tho Brahman
nearest. They it was who first knew the Spirit to bo
Brahman.

Com.—Because these Devas, Agni, Vâyu and Indra approached the Brahman nearest by conversing with and seeing That, they surpass the others considerably in the matter of power, quality and affluence. The particle '*Iva*' either has no meaning or has tho force of 'certainly'. Because these Devas, Agni, Vâyu and Indra approached nearest the most desirable Brahman, by such means as the conversation aforesaid, and because they were the first who knew the Brahman, they are foremost.

तस्माद्वा इन्द्रोऽतितरामिवान्यान्देवान्त होनद्विदिछं पस्पर्श स होनत्प्रथमो विदाञ्चकार ब्रह्मेति ॥ ३ ॥

3. Therefore also does Indra considerably excel other Devas because he approached Brahman nearest and because he first knew the Spirit to be Brahman.

Com.—Because even Agni and Vâyu knew Brahman from the words of Indra and because Indra first heard of the Brahman from the words of Uma, thoreforo does Indra so excel the other Devas. He approached Brahman nearest because he was the first who knew the Brahman.

तस्यैष आदेशो यदेतद्विद्युतो व्यद्युतदा उ इतीान्यर्मीमिषदा उ इत्यधिदेवतम् ॥ ४ ॥

4. Thus is That inculcated by illustration—that it flashed like lightning—that it appeared and vanished as the eye winketh. This is the illustration of the Brahman used in respect to the Devas.

Com.—Of the Brahman the subject discussed, this is the *Adésa. Adésa* is instruction by means of illustrations. The illustration by which the Brahman, the like of which does not exist, is explained is said to bo its *Adésa.* What is It? That which is well-known in the world as the flash of lightning. To add ' *krilaval* ' is inconsistent. Therefore we understand it to mean ' the flash of lightning '. The particle ' *A* ' means ' like '. The meaning is ' like the flash of lightning '. We find another Sruti saying ' As if a lightning flashed '. It just showed itself to the Devas like lightning and vanished from their view—or the word ' *Tejas* ' [bright] should be supplied after ' *Vidyulah* ' [of lightning]. The meaning then is that It shone for a moment like a dazzling flash of lightning. The word ' *iti* ' shows that it is an illustration. The word ' *ith* ' is used in the sense of ' and ' or ' else '. This is another illustration of it. What is it? It winked as the eye winks. The *nich* suffix has no distinct meaning from the meaning of the root. The particle ' *u* ' means ' like '. The meaning is that it was like the eye opening and closing to see and to turn from its objects. This illustration of the Brahman is taken from the activity of the deities.

अथाध्यात्मं यदेतद्गच्छतीव च मनोऽनेन चैतदुपस्मरत्यभीक्ष्ण
संकल्प: ॥ ५ ॥

5. Next illustration, from the Atman within the body—as speedily as the mind goes to Brahman—as speedily as one thinks of Brahman by the mind, and as speedily as the mind wills.

Com.—'*Atha*' means 'next'. We offer illustrations from the Atman within the body. 'Goes to' means 'perceives as an object'. As speedily as one (worshipper) thinks of the Brahman as near. '*Abhikshnam*' means 'very much'. 'Wills', *i.e.*, about the Brahman. By the volition, recollection of the mind, the Brahman as bounded by the mind is perceived as an object. Therefore this is an illustration of the Brahman taken from within the body, as lightning and winking from the activity of the powers. And as those illustrations show that Brahman flashes instantaneously, so these illustrations show that Brahman's appearance and disappearance are as quick as the perceptions of the mind. These illustrations of the Brahman are given because it can be understood by dull persons only if so illustrated. It is well known that the unconditioned Brahman can be known by persons of inferior intellect.

तद्ध तद्वनं नाम तद्वनमित्युपासितव्यं स य एतदेवं वेदाभि
हैनं सर्वाणि भूतानि संवाञ्छन्ति ॥ ६ ॥

6. The Brahman should be worshipped by all and
is hence called *Tadvana*. As *Tadvana*, It must be worshipped. Who thus knows Brahman, is loved by all
living beings.

Com.—' *Tat* ' means ' Brahman '. ' *Ha* ' means ' as is
well-known '. ' *Tadvanam* ' is a compound of *tat* and
vanam. It means 'which deserves to be worshipped
as the one Atman of all living things '. The Brahman
is well known as *Tadvanam* and should therefore be
worshipped as *Tadvana*, a word denoting its virtue.
' Worshipped ' means ' contemplated '. The Sruti next
declares the fruit attained by one who contemplates
the Brahman by this name. He who contemplates the
Brahman already defined as possessed of this virtue,
him (this worshipper) all living things love, i.e., pray
to him as they would to Brahman.

Thus instructed, the disciple addressed the preceptor
in the following manner.

उपनिषदं भो ब्रूहीत्युक्ता त उपनिषद्ब्राह्मीं वाव त उपनिषदमब्रू-
मेति ॥ ७ ॥

7. (The disciple). "(O Preceptor!) Teach me the
Upanishad". (The preceptor). " We have told thee the

11

Upanishad." " We have certainly told thee the Upanishad about Brahman."

Com.—When the disciple said "O holy one! Teach
me the secret that should be thought of", the preceptor
replied "the Upanishad has been taught thee." "What
is that Upanishad?". The preceptor replied "The Upanishad treating of Brahman, the supreme Self, has been
taught thee who excel in knowledge". The latter half
is introduced for decisively asserting that the knowledge of the supremo Paramâtman, the Brahman already
explained, is the Upanishad. Now what is the real
significance of the disciple, who has already heard
explained to him the knowledge of the Brahman,
asking the preceptor to tell him the Upanishad?. If the
question was about what was already explained, then
the question itself becomes redundant and meaningless
like *Pishtapeshana*. If however the Upanishad had
been only partially explained then the concluding it by
reciting its fruits : " Having turned away from this
world they become immortal," is not reasonable.
Therefore the question, if asked about the unexplained
portion of the Upanishad is also unsound, because there
was no portion yet to be explained. What then is the
meaning of the questioner?. We answer thus : The
disciple meant to say : " Does the Upanishad already
explained stand in need of anything else which should

combine with it to secure the desired end, or does it not stand in need of any such thing?. If it does, teach me the Upanishad about what is so required. If it does not, assert emphatically like Pippalâda in the words —There is nothing beyond this—." The preceptor's emphatical assertion, "The Upanishad has been told thee" is but proper. It may be said that this cannot be construed as an emphatic assertion, as already explained, for something yet had to be said by the preceptor. It is true that the preceptor adds '*Tasyi*', etc., but that is not added as a portion combining with the Upanishad already explained, in accomplishing the desired end, nor as a distinct aid for achieving the end with the Upanishad, but as something intended as a means to the acquisition of the knowledge of the Brahman; for *tapas*, etc., are apparently of the same importance with the Vedas and their supplements, being mentioned along with them. It is well known that neither the Vedas nor the supplements are the direct complements of the knowledge of the Brahman or concomitant helps to it. It is urged that it is only reasonable to assign different offices according to merit, even to many mentioned in the same breath. Just as the mantras for invoking the gods, where more than one is named, are used to perform the function of different deities according as the god to be invoked is this or that; it is urged it is to be inferred

that *tapas*, peace, *karma*, truth, eto., are either complements or concomitant helps to the knowledge of Brahman, and that the Vedas and their supplements, elu-
cidating meanings, are only helps to the knowledge of
karma and Atma. They urge that this distribution is
only reasonable from the reasonableness of the appli-
cability of their purport to this distribution. This cannot be, for it is illogical. This distinction is impossible
to bring about. It is unreasonable to think that the
knowledge of the Brahman, before which all notions of
distinctions of deed, doer, fruit, etc., vanish, can possibly require any extraneous thing as its complement
or concomitant aid in accomplishing it. Nor can its
fruit, emancipation, require any such. It is said: "One
desirous of emancipation should always renounce *karma* and all its aids. It is only by one that so renounces
that the highest place (can be reached).

Therefore knowledge cannot consistently with itself
require *karma* as its concomitant help or its complement. Therefore the distribution on the analogy of
the invocation in *Suktavâka* is certainly unsound.
Therefore it is sound to say that the question and
answer were intended only to make sure. The meaning
is "what was explained is all the Upanishad, which
does not require any thing else for ensuring emancipation."

तस्यै तपो दमः कर्मेति प्रतिष्ठा वेदाः सर्वाङ्गानि सत्यमाय-

तनम् ॥ ८ ॥

8.—Devotion, self-control and Karma are its pedestal, as also the Vedas and their supplements. Truth is its abode.

Com.—Of the Upanishad about Brahman which has been already taught, devotion, etc., are helps to the acquisition. '*Tapas*' means 'control of the body, the sensory organs and the mind'. '*Dama*' means 'freedom from passions.' 'Karma' is *Agnihôtra*, etc. It has been seen that knowledge of the Brahman arises indirectly through the purification of the mind in the person who has been refined by these. Even when Brahman is explained, those who have not been purged of their faults, either disbelieve or misbelieve in it as in the cases of Indra, Virôchana, etc. Therefore knowledge as inculcated arises only in him who has, by *tapas*, etc., performed either in this birth or in many previous ones, purified his mind. The Sruti says : "To that high-souled man whose devotion to the Lord is great and whose devotion to his preceptor is as great as that to the Lord, those secrets explained become illuminated." The Smriti says : " knowledge arises in men by annihilation of sinful deeds." The word '*iti*' is used to show that the mention of *tapas*, etc., is only by way of illustration; for it will show that there are other aids than those mentioned to the acquisition of knowledge, as freedom from pride, hatred of pomp, etc. '*Pratishta*' means 'legs.' For, when they exist, knowledge is firmly seated just as a person goes about with his legs, the four Vedas, all the six supplements, *i.e.*, *Siksha*, etc. The Vedas being the enlighteners of the knowledge of *karma* and the supplementary scriptures being intended for their protection are called 'legs' of the knowledge of Brahman. Or the word '*Pratishta*' having been construed as *legs*, the Vedas must be understood as all other parts of the body than the legs, such as the head, etc. In this case it should be understood that in the mention of Vedas the *Angás*, *sikshu*, etc., are in effect mentioned. When the trunk [*angi*] is mentioned, the limbs [*angás*] are included; because the limbs live in the trunk. The place where the Upanishad rests is Truth. 'Satyam' (Truth) means 'freedom from deceit and fraud in speech, mind or deed'; for, knowledge seeks those who are good-natured and free from deceit and not men of the nature of the Asuras and the deceitful; for, the Sruti says : ' Not in whom there is fraud, falsehood or deceit'. Therefore it is said that Truth is the resting place of knowledge. The mention again of Truth as the resting place of knowledge, notwithstand-

ing its implied mention as 'the leg on which knowledge
stands' along with devotion, etc., is to indicate that
Truth excels others as a help to knowledge; for, the
Smriti says : "If a thousand Aswamedha sacrifies and
Truth were weighed in the balance, one truth spoken
will outweigh the thousand saorifies."

योवा एतामेवं वेदापहृत्य पाप्मानमनन्ते स्वर्गे लोके ज्येये प्र-
तिरिष्ठति प्रतितिष्ठति ॥ ९ ॥

9. Ho who knows this thus, having shaken off all
sin, lives firmly seated in the endless, blissful and
highest Brahman. He lives firmly seated.

Com.—'This' means 'the knowledge of Brahman as
explained in '*keneshitam*', etc., and highly eulogised
in the text '*Brahmaha Devebhyo*', etc., and the source
of all knowledge. Although it has been already said
that by such knowledge one attains immortality, tho
fruit of the knowledge of Brahman is again stated at
the end. 'Sin' means 'the seed of *samsara*' whose
nature is ignorance, desire and *karma*'. '*Anante*'
means 'boundless'. '*Svarge loke*' means 'in the
Brahman who is all bliss' and not 'in heaven ' because
of the adjunct 'boundless '. It may be said that the
word 'boundless' is used in its secondary sense. Therefore the Sruti adds : 'Jyeye', 'highest of all'. The pur-

port is that he is firmly seated in the unconditioned Brahman, *i.e.*, does not again revert to *samsara* [worldly existence].

Thus ends the Commentary of Sri Sankara Charya.

————o————

Thus ends the Upanishad.

————o————

Mundakopanishad.

—o.—

Sri Sankara's Introduction.

—o—

OM TAT SAT.

—o—

Adoration to the Brahman. The *mantra* beginning with "Brahmâ Devânâm" ie one of the Athsrvana Upanishads. The Upanishad at its very commencement says how the knowledge therein contained was transmitted from preceptor to disciple and does this for the purpose of praising it. By showing how and with what great labor this knowledge was acquired by great sages as a means to secure the highest consummation, it extols knowledge to create a taste for it in the minds of the hearers; for, it is only when a taste for knowledge is created by praising it, they would eagerly seek to acquire it. How this knowledge is related to emancipation, as a means to its end, will be subsequently explained in the passages commencing with '*Bhidyate* etc.' Having first stated here that the knowledge, denoted by the word "Apara Vidya", such as Rig Veda etc., and consisting merely of mandatory and prohi-

12

bitory injunctions, cannot remove faults like ignorance etc., which are the cause of *Samsara* i.e., embodied existence and having, by the passages beginning with " *Avidyayâm antar vartamâna* " etc., shown a (marked) division of *Vidya* into *Para* and *Apara*, it explains in the passages beginning with ' *Parikshyu lôkan* etc.,' the knowledge of Brahman (*Brahmavidya*) which is a means to the attainment of the highest (*Para*) and which can be attained only by the grace of the preceptor, after a renunciation of the desire for all objects whether as means or ends. It also declares often the fruits of this knowledge in the passages " He who knows Brahman becomes Brahman itself" and " Having become Brahman while yet alive, all are freed." Although knowledge is permitted to all in any order of life, it is the knowledge of Brahman in a *Sanyâsin* that becomes the means of emancipation ; not the knowledge combined with *karma*. This is shown by such passages as " Living the life of a mendicant" and " Being in the order of the *Sanyâsin*" etc. This also follows from the antagonism between knowledge and *karma*; it is well known to be impossible that the knowledge of the identity of self with Brahman can be made to co-exist, even in a dream with *karma* (i. e., action). Knowledge being independent of time and not being the effect of definite causes cannot be limited by time.

If it be suggested that knowledge and *karma* can possibly co-exist as *indicated* by the fact that sages in the house-holder's order have handed down knowledge, we say that this mere indication (*linga*) cannot over-ride an obvious *fact*; for the co-existence of light and darkness cannot be brought about even by a hundred rules, much less by mere indications (*linga*) like these. A short commentary is now commenced of the Upanishad, whose relation to the end desired and whose result have been thus pointed out. This is named *Upanishad*; it may be either because it lessens the numerous evils of conception, birth, old age, disease etc., in persons who take kindly to this knowledge of Brahman and approach it with faith and devotion; or, because it makes them reach Brahman; or, because it totally destroys the cause of *samsâra*, such as ignorance etc.; thus from the several meanings of the root *shad* preceded by *upani*.

ओं । ब्रह्मा देवानां प्रथमः संबभूव विश्वस्यकर्ता भुवनस्य गोता ।
स ब्रह्मविद्यां सर्वविद्याप्रतिष्ठामथर्वाय ज्येष्ठपुत्राय प्राह ॥ १ ॥

Brahma was the first among the *devîs*, the creator of the universe, the protector of the world. He taught the knowledge of Brahman, on which all knowledge rests, to his eldest son Atharva.

Com.—The word "Brahma" means "much grown," "great", as excelling all others in virtue, knowledge, freedom from desires and power. The word *Devânâm* means Indra and others, literally, those possessing " enlightenment." The word ' Prathama' means " preeminent by attributes" or " at first." *Sambabhûva* means " became manifest well," *i.e.*, of free choice, not like mortals who are born in *samsâru*, in consequence of their good and bad deeds; for, the Smriti says " Ho who is beyond the reach of the senses and cannot be grasped etc." *Visvasya* means " of the whole universe." *Kurta*, ' creator'; *Bhuvanasya*, ' of the world' so created; *gôpta*, ' protector'; the epithets for Brahma are for eulogising the knowledge. He *i.e.*, Brahma whose greatness is thus celebrated. *Brahma Vidyám*, ' knowledge of the Brahman or tho Paramâtman' because it is described as knowledge ' by which one knows the undecaying and the true Purusha'; that knowledge is of the Paramâtman; or *Brahma Vidya* may mean " knowledge taught by Brahma the first born." *Sarva vidya pratishtam* means " that on which all knowledge rests for support"; because it is the cause of tho manifestation of all other knowledge; or, it may be, because the one entity to bo cognized by all knowledge is only known by this; for the Sruti says "by which, what is not heard becomes heard; what is not thought of becomes thought of; and what is not known becomes known." The expression " on which all knowledge depends " is also eulogy. He taught this knowledge to his eldest son; as Atharva was created at the beginning, in one of the numerous creations made by Brahma, he is said to be his eldest son. To him, his eldest son, he taught.

अथर्वणे यां प्रवेदत ब्रह्माथर्वा तां पुरोवाचाङ्गिरे ब्रह्मविद्यां ।

स भारद्वाजाय सत्यवहाय प्राह भारद्वाजोऽङ्गिरसे परावराम् ॥२॥

That knowledge of Brahman which Brahma taught to Atharva, Atharva taught to Angira in ancient days; and he taught it to one of the Bhâradvâja family by name Satyavaha; and Satyavaha taught to Angiras the knowledge so descended from the greater to the less.

Com.—That knowledge of the Brahman which Brahma taught to Atharva, the same knowledge thus acquired from Brahma, Atharva in ancient days taught to one named *Angih*; and this *Angih* taught it to one named Satyavaha of the line of the Bhâradvâja; and Bhârad-vâja taught it to Angiras, his disciple or his son. *Para-varâm*, because it was acquired from superior by inferior sages; or, because it permeates the subject of all knowledge, great and small; the term *Prâha, i.e., taught* should be read into the last clause.

शौनको ह वै महाशालोऽङ्गिरसं विधिवदुपसन्नः पप्रच्छ ।

कस्मिन्नु भगवो विज्ञाते सर्वमिदं विज्ञातं भवतीति ॥ ३ ॥

Saunaka, a great *grihasta*, having duly approached Angiras, questioned him " What is that, O Bhagavan, which being known, all this becomes known".

Com.—Saunaka, the male issue of Sunaka. *Muhá-sálám* means "the great house-holder"; Angiras *i. e.*, the disciple of Bháradvája and his own preceptor; *Vidhival* means 'duly'; *i.e.*, according to the *sastras*; *Upasannah* means 'having approached'; *Paprachcha* means 'quostioned'; from "*the approaching duly*" men-tioned just after the connection between Saunaka and Angiras, it should be inferred that in respect of the manner of approaching, there was no established rule among the ancients, before him. The attribute "duly" might have been intended either to fix a limit, or to apply to all aliko, on the analogy of a lamp placed amidst a house; for the rule about "the manner of ap-proaching" is intended in the case of persons like us also. What did he say? " What is that? Oh Bhaga-van etc." The particle *nu* expresses doubt. *Bhagavo* means 'O Bhagavan'. "All this" means " everything knowable". *Vijnátam* means 'specially known or under-stood.' [Oh Bhagavn, what is that which being known overything knowable becomes well-known]. Saunaka, having heard the saying of good men that "when one is known, ho becomes the knower of all," and being desirous of knowing that one in particular, asked in

doubt "what is that etc."; or, having seen merely from
a popular view, questioned. There are in the world
varieties of pieces of gold etc., which, though different
are known by people in the world by the knowledge of
the unity of the substance (gold etc.); similarly "Is
there one cause of all the varieties in the world, which
cause being known, all will be well-known."? It may be
said that when the existence of the thing is not known,
the question "what is that etc.," is not appropriate and
the question in the form " is there etc.," would then be
appropriate; if the existence is established, the question
may well be "what is that etc.," as in the expression,
"With whom shall it be deposited." The objection is
unsound; the question in this form is appropriate from
fear of troubling by verbosity.

तस्मै स होवाच । द्वे विद्ये वेदितव्य इति ह स्म यद्ब्रह्मविदो
वदन्ति परा चैवापराच ॥ ४ ॥

To him he said "There are two sorts of knowledge to
be acquired. So those who know the Brahman say;
namely, *Para* and *Apara*, *i.e.*, the higher and the lower.

Com.—Angiras said to Saunaka. What did he say?.
(He said) that there were two sorts of knowledge to be
known. So indeed, do those who know the import of
the Vedas and who see the absolute truth, say what
these two sorts are; he says: *Para* is the knowledge of

the Paramâtman and *Apara* is that which deals with
the means and the results of good and bad actions. It
may be asked how, having to say what it was that
Saunaka asked about in the question—" What being
known one becomes omniscient ", Angiras stated what
he was not asked about, by the passage " there are two
sorts of knowledge etc." This is no fault; for the reply
requires this order of statement. *Apara vidya* is ignorance and that ought to be dispelled. When what is
known is *Apara vidya*, i.e., the subject of ignorance,
nothing can be known as it is. The rule is that after
thus refuting the faulty theory, the true conclusion
should be stated.

तत्रापरा ऋग्वेदो यजुर्वेदः सामवेदोऽथर्ववेदः शिक्षा कल्पो व्या-
करणं निरुक्तं छन्दो ज्योतिषमिति ।
अथ परा यया तदक्षरमधिगम्यते ॥ ५ ॥

Of these, the Apara is the Rig Veda, the Yajur Veda,
the Sama Veda, and the Atharva Veda, the *siksha*, the
code of rituals, grammar, *nirukta, chchandas* and astrology. Then the *para* is that by which the immortal is
known.

Com.—Of these, what Aparavidya is, is explained.
Rig Veda, Yajur Veda, Sama Veda and the Atharva
Veda, these four Vedas, the *siksha*, the code of rituals,

grammar, *nirukta, chchandas* and astrology, these six *angas* (of Vedas), all this is knowledge called *Apara* ; now, knowledge called *Para* is explained. It is that by which the "immortal" as hereafter described is reached; for, the root *gam*, with *adhi* before it, generally means *reach*. Nor is the attainment of the highest, different from the sense of knowledge. The attainment of the highest is merely the removal of ignorance. They mean the same thing. It may be asked how that Vidya could be called *para* and a help to emancipation, if such Vidya be excluded by the Rig Veda etc; for, the Smriti says "Those Smritis which are excluded by the Vedas etc." It will become unacceptable, because it sees wrongly and leads to no good results ; and again the Upanishads will become excluded by the Rig Veda etc., but if they are included in the Rig Veda, etc., a separate classification is useless. How then can it be called *para* ?. The objection has no force; for by the term "Vidya" is here meant the *knowledge* of a subject ; by the term "Para Vidya" is meant primarily in this context, that *knowledge* of the immortal which could be known through the Upanishads and *not the mere assemblage of words* in them ; but by the term *Vidya* is always understood the assemblage of words forming it. As the immortal cannot be realised by a mere mastery of the assemblage of words without other

13

efforts, such as the approaching a preceptor and spurning all desires etc, the separate classification of the knowledge of Brahman and its designation as *para vidya* are proper.

यत्तदद्रेश्यमग्राह्यमगोत्रमवर्णमचक्षुःश्रोत्रं तदपाणिपादम् ।
नित्यं विभुं सर्वगतं सुसूक्ष्मं तदव्ययं यद्भूतयोनिं परिपश्यन्ति धीराः ॥

That which cannot be perceived, which cannot be seized, which has no origin, which has no properties, which has neither ear nor eye, which has neither hands nor feet, which is eternal, diversely manifested, all-pervading, extremely subtle, and undecaying, which the intelligent cognized as the source of the *Bhûtas*.

Com.—As in the matter of an injunction (*vidhi*) there is something *to be done*, as of the nature of Agnihôtra etc, subsequent to the realization of its import, with the aid of many requisites (*kâraka*), such as the doer etc, there is nothing here *to be done* in the matter of the knowledge of the Brahman. It is accomplished simultaneously with the realization of the import of the text; for, there is nothing here except being centred in the knowledge revealed by mere words. Therefore, the *Para vidya* is here explained with reference to Brahman, as described in the text " that which cannot be perceived etc."; what is to be explained is realized in the mind and referred to, as what is already known by the expression "that which"; *Adrisyam* means 'that cannot be perceived', invisible, *i.e.*, beyond the reach of all the intellectual senses; for, vision externally directed is the medium for the working of the five senses. *Agrâhyam* means 'that cannot be seized,' *i.e.*, not an object for the organs of action. *Gôtram* means 'line or source'; therefore *Agôtram* means 'unconnected with anything', for it has no source with which it can be connected. *Varnah* means "those which are described," *i e.*, properties of objects such as bigness etc., whiteness etc.; *avarnam*, 'that which has no properties'; the eye and the ear are organs found in all animals perceiving name and form. It is said to be *Achakshu srôtram*, because it has not these organs. From the attribute of intelligence, as inferred from the text "who knows all and everything of each", it may be thought that it accomplishes its purpose, like people in *samsâra*, with the aid of organs such as the eye, the ear etc. This supposition is here avoided by the expression "having neither eye nor ear"; for, the texts "he sees without eyes" and "hears without ears" etc., are found; moreover, it has neither hands nor feet, *i.e.*, has no organs of action; thus, as it is neither grasped nor grasps, it is *nitya*, *i.e.*, immortal. *Vibhum*, because it is diversely manifested in the form of living things,

from Brahma down to the immovable. *Sarvagatam*,
i.e., all-pervading like the *ákás*. *Susúkshmam, i.e.*,
extremely subtle, because there is no cause like sound
to make it gross; for, it is sound and the rest that are
the causes *seriatim* of the greater and greater grossness
of the *ákás*, wind and the rest; as they do not exist
here, it is very subtle; again, it is *avyayam, i.e.*, undecaying, because of its being what it was just stated to
be; it does not decay, therefore it is undecaying; for
decay consisting in the diminution of limbs, as in the
case of a body, is not possible in what has no limbs; nor
is 'decay' consisting in the diminution of treasure
possible as in the case of a king; nor is 'decay' in
respect of attributes possible, because it has no attributes and is itself all. *Yat*, answering to this description.
Bhútayônim, the source of all created things or elements,
as earth is of all that is immovable and movable.
Paripasyanti, see everywhere the Atman of all, *i.e.*, the
immortal Dhírah, the intelligent, *i. e.*, those possessed
of discernment; that knowledge by which this immortal Brahman is known is what is called Paravidya;
this is the drift of the whole.

यथोर्णनाभिः सृजते गृह्णते च यथा पृथिव्यामोषधयः संभवन्ति ।

यथा सतः पुरुषात्केशलोमानि तथाऽक्षरात्संभवतीह विश्वम् ॥ ७ ॥

As the spider creates and absorbs, as medicinal plants grow from the earth, as hairs grow from the living person, so this universe proceeds from the immortal.

Cóm.—It was said the immortal is the source of all created things. How it is the source is explained by well-known analogies; as is well-known in the world, the spider without requiring any other cause itself creates, *i. e.*, sends out threads not distinct from its own body and again absorbs them itself, *i. e.*, draws them into itself or makes them part of itself; as medicinal plants, *i. e.*, from the corn plant to the immovable, not distinct from the earth, proceed from the earth, and as from the living person the hairs proceed different in nature from him ; as in these illustrations, so here, *i. e.*, in the circle of *samsára*, all the universe of the same and different nature proceeds from the *akshara* above described, without requiring any other cause ; the statement of many analogies is to facilitate easy understanding of the meaning ; universe which proceeds from the Brahman proceeds in this order and not all at once, like the throwing of a handful of apples.

तपसा चीयते ब्रह्म ततोऽन्नमभिजायते ।

अन्नात्प्राणो मनः सत्यं लोकाः कर्मसु चामृतम् ॥ ८ ॥

By *tapas* Brahman increases in size and from it food

is produced; from food the *prâna*, the mind, the Bhûtas the worlds, *karma* and with it, its fruits.

Com.—This *mantra* is begun for the purpose of stating the fixed order of creation. 'By *tapas*,' by knowledge of how to create the Brahman which is the source of all created things; 'increases,' *i. e.*, becomes distended, being desirous to create the world as a seed when sending out the sprout, or as a father desirous of begetting a son dilates with joy; from the Brahman thus extended by its omniscience, *i. e.*, by its knowledge and its power of creation, preservation and destruction of the universe; *Annam* means 'that which is eaten or enjoyed', *i. e.*, the unmanifested (*avyákritam*) common to all in *samsâra* is produced in the state fit for emancipation; and from "the unmanifested", *i. e.*, the "Annam" in the state fit for manifestation. *Prana, i. e.*, Hiranyagarbha, the common cosmic entity, endowed with the power of knowledge and activity of the Brahman, the sprouting seed, as it were, of the totality of cosmic ignorance, desire, *karma*, and creatures and the Atman of the universe. "Is produced", should be supplied. From that *prâna*, that which is called "mind" whose characteristic is volition, deliheration, doubt, determination etc., is produced; aud from that mind whose essence is volition etc., what is called *satyam, i. e.*, the five elements such as the *âkâs* etc., is produced and from the five elements called *satya*, the seven worlds, the earth etc., are produced in the order of the globes ; and in them *karma*, for the living beings, man etc., according to caste and the order of life, is produced; and with *karma* as the cause, its fruits. As long as *karma* is not destroyed, even by hundreds of millions of *kalpa*, so long is its fruit not destroyed. Hence it is called *Amritam*.

य: सर्वज्ञः सर्वविद्यस्य ज्ञानमयं तपः ।

तस्मादेतद्ब्रह्म नाम रूपमन्नं च जायते ॥ ९ ॥

From the Brahman who knows all and everything of all and whose *tapas* is in the nature of knowledge, this Brahma, name, form and food are produced.

Com.—By way of concluding what was already stated the *mantra* says as follows : 'Yah,' above described and named *akshara* ; *Sarvajna* means he who knows all, who knows all things as a class. *Sarvavid, i.e.*, who knows everything in particular; whose *tapas* is only a modification of knowledge, consists in omniscience and is not in the nature of modification. From him so described, omniscient, this, *i. e.*, manifested Brahman, by name Hiranyagarbha, is produced. Again name, such as ' This is Devadatta, and Yajnadatta etc.'; and form such as 'this is white, blue etc.,' and food

such as corn, *yava* etc., are produced in the order
stated in the last text; thus there is no inconsistency.

————o————

Here ends the commentary
on the first part of the
first Mundaka.

————o————

Mundakopanishad.

तदेतत्सत्यं मन्त्रेषु कर्माणि कवयो यान्यपश्यंस्तानि त्रेतायां बहुधा
सन्ततानि ।

तान्याचरथ नियतं सत्यकामा एप वः पन्थाः सुकृतस्य लोके ॥१॥

The various *karma* which seers found in the *mantras* are true and were much practised in the *Treta* age; practise them always with true wishes. This is your way to the attainment of the fruits of *karma*.

Com.—By the text the Rig Veda, the Yajur Veda etc., all Vedas with their *angas* (appendages) have been stated to be *apara vidya* ; and *para vidya* has been specifically stated to be that knowledge by which the *akshara* described in the text beginning with "That which cannot be perceived etc.," and ending with "Name, form and food are produced", is known. Hereafter the next text is begun to distinguish between the bondage of *samsara* and emancipation, the

14

subjects of these two sorts of knowledge respectively.
Of these, the subject of *Apara viyda* is *samsára* which
consists in the variety of action, its means such as doer
etc., and its results, is without beginning or end, and
being misery in its naturo should be discarded by every
embodied being; and in its entirety it is of an unbro-
ken connection like the stream of a river.   The subject
of *para vidya* is emancipation which consists in the ces-
sation of *sumsara*, which is beginning-less, endless, undecaying, immortal, deathless, fearless, pure and clear and
is nothing but being centred in self and transcendant
bliss without a second; first it is attempted to elucidate
the subject of *apara vidya*; for, it is only when it is seen
that it is possible to get disgusted with it; accordingly
it will be said later on "Having examined the world
attained by *karma*"; and as there can be no examination
of what is not presented to the view, the text shows
what it is. '*Satyam*,' 'true.' What is that? *Muntreshu*,
in the Vedas known as Rig, Yajur, etc. '*Karmani*,'
Agnihólra and the rest disclosed by texts of the Vedas;
'*Kavayah*,' 'seers like Vasishtha and others'. '*Apasyan*'
have seen. This is true because they are the unfailing
means of accomplishing the objects of man. These enjoined by the Vedas and seen by the Rishis were done
in diverse ways by the followers of *karma*. *Treldyám*,
i. e., wherein there is the combination of the three

Vedas of the three modes of rites performed with the
aid of a *hota*, *adhvaryu* and *udgata*, or it may mean
that they were generally performed in the *Treta* age.
Therefore you should do them always; '*Satyakamah*'
'wishing for those fruits which they can bear'. This is
your route for the attainment of the fruits of *Karma*.
Sukritasya, performed by you ; *Loka* is what is found,
or enjoyed ; hence the fruits of *karma* are denoted by
the word " Loka". The meaning is that, to attain them
this is the route. These *karma*, *Agnihotra* and the rest
enjoined in the Vedas form the road, *i. e.*, the means for
the attainment of the necessary fruits.

यदा लेलायते ह्याचिं: समिद्धे हव्यवाहने ।

तदाज्यभागावन्तरेणाहुती: प्रतिपादयेत् ॥ २ ॥

When the flame of the fire burning high is moving,
then one should perform the oblations in the space between the portions, where the ghee should be poured
on either side.

Com.—Of the various kinds of *karma*, *agnihotra* is first explained to show what it is, because
it is the first of all *karma*. How is that to be
performed?. When the flame moves, the fire being well
fed by fuel, then in the flame so moving between the
portions where quantities of ghee are poured on either

side, *i. e.*, in the place called *arapasthana* one should throw the oblations intending them for the *devata*. As the same has to be done during many days the plural *oblations* is used. This *karma marga* which consists in properly offering the oblations etc., is the road to the attainment of good worlds but it is not easy to do that properly and the impediments are many.

यस्याग्निहोत्रमदर्शमपौर्णमासमचातुर्मास्यमनाग्रयणमतिथिवर्जितं च ।
अहुतमवैश्वदेवमाविधिना हुतमासतमांस्तस्य लोकान्हिनस्ति ॥३॥

He whose *agnihotra* is without *Darsa*, without *paurnamasa*, without *Chathurmasya*, without *agrayana*, without *atithi* (guests) and without oblation is without *vaisvadeva*, or irregularly performed, destroys his worlds till the seventh.

Com.—How is that so ?. 'Without Darsa', without ritual named *Darsa*, for, one who performs *agnihotra* should necessarily perform *Darsa*; though connected with *agnihotra* (as a part of it) it becomes as it were an attribute of *agnihotra*. The drift is *Agnihotra* without *Darsa* performed. The expressions " without *Paurnamasa* etc.," as attributes of *agnihotra* should be similarly noted; for all are equally the *angas* (parts) of *agnihotra*. 'Without *Paurnamasa*', devoid of the *Paurnamasa* ritual. 'Without *Chathurmasya*', devoid of the *chathurmasya* ritual. 'Without *agrayana*', dovoid of tho *agrayana* ritual which is to be performed in autumn etc.; similarly 'without *atithi*,' devoid of the daily propitiation of guests ; '*ahutam*', oblation not offered well by himself at the time for *agnihotra*. "Without *raisvadera*", like "without *Darsa*", *means* dovoid of tho *vaisvadeva* ritual. Is ' irregularly performed,' oblation though offered, not offered in the proper manner. What such *karma*, as *agnihotra* ill-performed or not performed at all, leads to, is stated immediately after. 'Till tho seventh', inclusive of the seventh. 'His,' of the doer. ' Destroys tho seven worlds of tho doer', seems to destroy ; because only the trouble taken is the fruit ; for it is only when *karma* is properly performed, the seven worlds beginning with *Bhú* and ending with *satya* are obtained as result, according to the fruition of tho *karma*. These worlds are not obtainable by *agnihotra* and other *karma*, performed as just above stated and they are therefore said to be as it were destroyed ; but tho more trouble is ever present ; or it may be construed to mean that tho three ancestors (the father, the grand-father and the great-grand-father) and tho three decendants (the son, the grandson and the' great-grandson) connected by the offer of oblations do not confer any benefit on his soul by virtue of the *agnihotra* and the rest, performed as above stated.

काली कराली च मनोजया च सुलोहिता या च सुधूम्रवर्णा।
स्फुलिङ्गिनी विश्वरुची च देवी लेलायमाना इति सप्त जिह्वाः ॥

Kali, karáli, also *manojava, sulohita, sudhúmravarna, sphulingini,* and *visvaruchi* are the seven moving tongues of fire.

Com.—The seven tongues of the (flaming) fire, from *kali* down to *visvaruchi,* are intended to swallow the oblations thrown on it.

एतेषु यश्चरते भ्राजमानेषु यथाकालं चाहुतयोह्याददायन् ।
तन्नयन्त्येताः सूर्यस्य रश्मयो यत्र देवानां पतिरेकोऽधिवासः ॥५॥

Him who performed *karma* (*agnihotra*) in the bright flames at the proper time, these oblations, performed by him, conduct through the rays of the sun where the Lord of the Devas is sole sovereign.

Com.—The *agnihotri* who performs the *karma, agnihotra* and the rest, in these different bright tongues of the fire, at the time fixed for the performance of the *karma* these oblations (performed by him) becoming so many rays of the sun conduct him to Heaven, where Indra, Lord of the Devas, singly rules over all. '*Adakáyan,*' taking (the sacrificer).

एह्येहीति तमाहुतयः सुवर्चसः सूर्यस्य रश्मिभिर्यजमानं वहन्ति ।
प्रियां वाचमभिवदन्त्योऽर्चयन्त्य एष वः पुण्यः सुकृतो ब्रह्मलोकः ॥६।

These oblations shining bright carry the sacrificer through the rays of the sun bidding him welcome, propitiating him and greeting him with pleasing words. This is the well-laid path of virtue leading to *Brahmaloka.* .

Com.—How these carry the sacrificer through the sun's rays is now explained; calling " come, como," these bright oblations greeting him with pleasant words, i. e., with words of praise etc., and propitiating him, i. e., addressing him with such pleasing words, as " this is your virtuous and well-laid road to *Brahmaloka,* the fruits of your deeds". The word *Brahmaloka* by the force of the context means " *Svarga* or Heaven ".

प्लवा ह्येते अदृढा यज्ञरूपा अष्टादशोक्तमवरं येषु कर्म ।
एतच्छ्रेयो येऽभिनंदन्ति मूढा जरामृत्युं ते पुनरेवापि यन्ति ॥ ७ ॥

The eighteen persons necessary for the performance of sacrifice are transitory and not permanent and *karma* in its nature inferior, has been stated as resting upon these. Those ignorant persons who delight in this, as leading to bliss, again fall into decay and death.

Com.—This *karma,* devoid of knowledge, bears but this much fruit and being · accomplished by ignorance, desire and action, is sapless and is the source of misery. Therefore it is condemned. " *Plava* "

means 'ephemeral' because these are *adridha*, *i. e.*, not
permanent. *Yajnarûpa*, the forms of sacrifice, *i.e.*,
necessary for tho performance of the sacrifice. Eighteen in number, consisting of tho sixteen *Ritviks*,
the sacrificer and his wife. Karma stated in the *sastras*
depends on theso. *Avaram karma i. e.*, mere *karma*
devoid of knowledge ; and as the performance of *karma*
which is inferior depends on these eighteen who are not
permanent. The *karma* done by them and its fruit are
ephemeral, as, when the pot is destroyed, the destruction
of milk, curd etc. in it, follows. This being so, those
ignorant persons who delight in this *karma* as the
means of bliss, fall again into decay and death after
staying sometime in Heaven.

अविद्यायामन्तरे वर्तमाना: स्वयं धीरा: पण्डितं मन्यमाना: ।

जङ्घन्यमाना: परियन्ति मूढा अन्धेनैव नीयमाना यथान्धा: ॥८॥

Being in the midst of ignorance and thinking in
their own minds that they are intelligent and learned,
tho ignorant wander, afflicted with troubles, like the
blind led by the blind.

Com.—Moreover, being in the midst of ignorance,
i. e., being utterly ignorant and thinking in their
own minds "we alone are intelligent and have
known all that should be known." Thus flatter-
ing themselves, the ignorant wander, much afflicted

by old age, sickness and a lot of other troubles, being devoid of vision as the blind in this world, going the way pointed out by persons, themselves blind, fall into ditch and brambles.

अविद्यायां बहुधा वर्तमाना वयं कृतार्थी इत्यभिमन्यन्ति बाला: ।
यत्कर्मिणो न प्रवेदयन्ति रागात्तेनातुरा: क्षीणलोकाश्च्यवन्ते ॥९॥

The ignorant following the diverse ways of ignorance, flatter themselves that their objects have been accomplished. As these followers of *karma* do not learn the truth owing to their desire, they grow miserable and after the fruits of their *karma* are consumed, fall from Heaven.

Com.—The ignorant acting diversely according to ignorance, flatter themselves that they have achieved what they should. This being so, the followers of *karma* do not learn the truth as they are assailed with the desire for the fruits of *karma* ; they grow miserable for that reason and fall from heaven after the fruits of their *karma* are consumed.

इष्टापूर्तं मन्यमाना वरिष्ठं नान्यच्छ्रेयो वेदयन्ते प्रमूढा: ।
नाकस्य पृष्ठे ते सुकृतेऽनुभूत्वेमं लोकं हीनतरं वा विशन्ति ॥१०॥

These ignorant men regarding sacrificial and charitable acts as most important, do not know any other help to bliss ; having enjoyed in the heights of Heaven the

15

abode of pleasures, they enter again into this or even inferior world.

.*Com.*—"*Ishtam*," *karma* enjoined by the Srutis as sacrifies, etc. "*Pûrtham*," *karma* enjoined by Smritis such as the digging of pools, wells, tanks etc. Regarding these alone as the most important aids to the attainment of human objects, these ignorant men, being infatuated with attachment to their sons, cattle and relatives, do not know the other called ' knowledge of self' which is the help to bliss.   Having enjoyed in the top of heaven—the place of pleasures—the fruits of their *karma*, they enter again into this world of men or even inferior world, such as the world of horizontal beings, hell, etc., according to the residue of their *karma*.

तपःश्रद्धे ये ह्युपवसन्त्यरण्ये शान्ता विद्वांसो भैक्षचर्यां चरन्तः ।
सूर्यद्वारेण ते विरजाः प्रयान्ति यत्रामृतः स पुरुषो ह्यव्ययात्मा

॥ ११ ॥

But they who perform *tapas* and *sruddha* in the forest, having a control over their senses, learned and living the life of a mendicant, go through the orb of the sun, their good and bad deeds consumed, to where the immortal and undecaying *Purusha* is.

Com.—But those who possess the knowledge contrary to that of persons previously mentioned, *i.e.*, the hermits of the forest and the *Sanyasins*. '*Tapah*,' the *karma* enjoined on one's order of life. '*Sraddha*,' the worship of the *Hiranyagarbha* and other deities. *Uparasanti*,' follow. '*Aranye*', living in the forest. '*Sântâh*,' having control over the group of senses. 'Learned' includes also house-holders who possess chiefly knowledge, living by begging; because, they have nothing to call their own. 'Living on alms' is connected with 'living in the forest.' 'Through the orb of the sun,' through the northern route indicated by the sun. 'Virajâh,' their good and bad deeds being consumed. 'Prayânti,' go with excellence. 'Where,' to *Satyaloka* where the immortal *Purusha*, the first born, undecaying *Hiranyagarbha* is. 'Undecaying,' because he lives to the end of *samsara*. With this, end the movements within the pale of *samsara* attainable, through *aparavidya*. If it be said that some regard this as emancipation, we say it is not so because of the Srutis, 'All his desires are even here absorbed' and 'those intelligent persons whose mind is concentrated reach the all-pervading, on all sides and enter into everything, etc.,' and because of the mention of emancipation being irrelevant in this context; for, in the course of treating of the *aparavidya*, there is no pertinency of emancipation being brought in. The consumption of *karma* spoken of is only relative; all the result of the *aparavidya* be-

ing in the nature of ends and means and diversified by
tho differenco of acts, requisites and fruits and partak-
ing of duality is only this much, which ends with reaching *Hiranyagarbha*. Accordingly also it has been
said by Manu speaking of the various stages within
samsara from the inmovable upwards: 'The wise con-
sider this a high and pure stage to attain the world of
Brahma, tho *Prajapatis* (creators), virtue, *mahat* and
aryakta.'

परीक्ष्य लोकान्कर्मचितान्ब्राह्मणो निर्वेदमायान्नास्त्यकृतः कृतेन ।
तद्विज्ञानार्थं स गुरुमेवाभिगच्छेत्समित्पाणिः श्रोत्रियं ब्रह्मनिष्ठम्॥ १२॥

Let a Brahmin having examined the worlds produced by *karma* be free from desires thinking, 'there is
nothing eternal produced by *karma* '; and in order to
acquire the knowledge of tho eternal, let him *Samid*
(sacrificial fuel) in hand, approach a preceptor alone,
who is versed in the Vedas and centred in the Brahman.

Com.—Now this is said for the purpose of showing
that only the person thoroughly disgusted with all
samsara which is in the nature of ends and means, is
entitled to acquire the *para vidya*. ' *Parikshya*', well
knowing that the subject of *apara vidya* consisting of
the Rig, and other Vedas, performable by a person
tainted with the defects of natural ignorance, desires

and *karma* has been intended for a person possessed of such defects and after examining those worlds which are the fruits of such *karma* performed, attainable by the northern and southern routes and these others such as Hell, the world of beasts and the world of departed spirits, which are the result of the vices of not performing the prescribed *karma* and performing the forbidden *karma*; after having examined these worlds with the aid of experience, inference, analogies and *ágamas*, i. e., determined the true nature of all these worlds attainable by one within the pale of *samsara*, beginning from the *avyakta* down to the immovable, manifested and unmanifested in their nature, productive of each other like the seed and its sprout, agitated by a hundred thousand troubles, fragile like the womb of the plantain, similar in kind to illusion, the waters of the mirage, the shape of cities formed by the clouds in the sky, dreams, water-bubbles and foam and destroyed every moment and discarding all these as being produced by good and bad deeds and acquired by *karma* induced by the faults of ignorance and desire. The word '*Bráhmana*' is here used because the Brahmin is specially competent to acquire the knowledge of Brahman through wholesale renunciation. What he should do after examining these worlds is explained. '*Nirvedam*,' the root *vid* with the prefix *nih* is here used in the sense of freedom from desires. The meaning is that he will get disgusted. The mode of disgust is thus shown: ' Here,' in *samsara* there is nothing which is not made; for, all worlds produced by *karma* are transitory. The meaning is : there is nothing eternal; for all *karma* is help to what is merely transitory. All that is produced by *karma* is one of four kinds, that which is produced, that which is reached, that which is refined and that which is modified; beyond this nothing can be done by *karma*. But I am a seeker after that consummation which is eternal, immortal, fearless, changeless, immovable and constant; but not after one of a contrary nature; of what use therefore is *karma* which is full of trouble and which leads to misery?. Thus disgusted, the Brâhmin should, for knowing that abode which is fearless, full of bliss, not made, and eternal, only approach a preceptor, possessing attributes such as control of mind, control of the external senses and mercy etc., (the force of the word 'alone' is to show that even one versed in the recital of the *sastras* should not independently by himself seek the knowledge of the Brahman) with a load of *samid* in his hand. ' *Srotriyam*,' versed in the recital of the Vedas and the knowledge of its import. ' *Brahmanishtham* ;' like *japunishtha* and *taponishtha*, this word means ' one who is centred in the Brahman devoid of attributes and 'without a second, after renouncing all *karma* ; for, one performing *karma* cannot be centred in the Brahman on account of the antagonism between *karma* and the knowledge of the Atman.   Having duly approached the *guru*, let the Brāhmin propitiate him and question him about the true and immortal *Purusha*.

तस्मै स विद्वानुपसन्नाय सम्यक्प्रशान्तचित्ताय शामान्यिताय ।
येनाक्षरं पुरुषं वेद सत्यं प्रोवाच तां तत्वतो ब्रह्मविद्याम् ॥१ ३॥

To him who has thus approached, whose heart is well subdued and who has control over his senses, let him truly teach that *Brahmavidya* by which the true immortal *purusha* is known.

Oom—'Ho,' the learned preceptor who knows the Brahman; '*Upasannaya*,' who has approached him. '*Samyak*,' i. e., well, according to the *sastras*; '*Prasánta chiththáya*,' i. e., whose heart is subdued, who is free from such faults as pride etc. '*Samánvitáya*,' who has control also over the external senses, i. e., who has turned away from everything in the world. 'By which knowledge,' by the *para vidya*. '*Aksharam*,' that which has been described as imperceivable etc., and denoted by the word *Purusha*, because it is all-pervading; or, because it is seated in the city of the body. '*Satyam*,' the same because it is truth in its nature. '*Akshara*,' because it knows no decay, because it is scathless, and because it knows no destruction. ‘Veda’ means ‘know.’ The meaning is ‘let him teach that knowledge of the Brahman as it should be taught. This is the duty of also the preceptor, that he should make the good pupil duly approaching him, cross the sea of ignorance.

———o———

Here ends the commentary on
the second part of the
First Mundaka.

———o———

Here ends the First Mundaka.

———o———

SECOND

𝕸𝖚𝖓𝖉𝖆𝖐𝖔𝖕𝖆𝖓𝖎𝖘𝖍𝖆𝖉.

---o---

PART I.

---o---

तदेतत्सत्यं यथा सुदीप्तात्पावकाद्विस्फुलिङ्गाः सहस्रशः प्रभवन्ते
सरूपाः ।

तथाक्षराद्विविधाः सौम्य भावाः प्रजायन्ते तत्र चैवापि यन्ति ॥१॥

This is true ; as from the flaming fire issue forth, by
thousands, sparks of the same form, so from the immortal proceed, good youth, diverso *jivas* and they find their
way back into it.

Com.—Everything made, as the result of *apara vidya*
has already been stated. That entity known as *Purusha* from which *samsara* derives its strength, from
which, as its immortal source, it proceeds and into
which it is again absorbed is true ; the subsequent
portion of the book is begun for the purpose of explain-
ing him, who being known, all will become known and
who is the subject of 'Brahmavidya.' The *satyam* or
truth which is the subject of the *apara vidya* and which

16

is in the nature of the fruits of *karma* is only relatively true; but this which is the subject of *para vidya*
is absolutely true, being defined as absolute existence.
This *satyam* is real, being the subject of knowledge;
the other *satyam* is false, being the subject of ignorance. How could men directly cognize the immortal
and real *Purusha* seeing that it is altogether beyond
the reach of direct perception. To this end, the Sruti
gives an example: 'As from the fire well-fed sparks,
i.e., particles of fire issue forth by thousands, like fire
in their form; so, from the immortal above described
diverse *jivas*, diverse because of the difference of conditions, *i.e.*, in their various bodies, come into existence.
Just as from *ákás*, the spaces enclosed as it were within the limits of a pot, etc.' As these spaces undergo
varieties corresponding to the varieties of their conditions such as pot etc., so also the *jivas* according to the
varieties of their bodies created by names and forms.
The *jivas* are absorbed into the immortal *purusha* when
the bodies conditioning them cease to exist, as the
various cavities cease to exist, when the pot, etc.,
cease to exist. As the origin and destruction of the
various cavities in the *ákás* are due to its being enclosed in a pot, etc., so also the cause and the absorption of the *jiva* are due to the *akshara* being conditioned by bodies bearing names and forms.

दिव्यो ह्यमूर्तः पुरुषः सवाह्याभ्यन्तरो ह्यजः ।
अप्राणो ह्यमनाः शुभ्रो ह्यक्षरात्परतः परः ॥ २ ॥

He is bright, formless, all-pervading, existing without and within, unborn, without *prâna*, without mind,
pure and beyond the *avyâkrita*, which is beyond all.

Com.—With n view to describe the nature of that
akshara, *i.e.*, which is beyond what is known as *avyákrita* (the unmanifested) the seed of all name and form
and transcending its own modifications which is devoid
of all varieties of conditions and bereft of all forms like
the *âkás* and which is capable of being only negative-
ly defined, the text says thus. '*Divyah*', bright, being
self-resplendent, or born of itself or distinct from all
that is worldly. ' Hi', because ; '*amúrtah*,' having uo
form of any kind. '*Purusha*,' all-pervading or seated
in the city of the body. '*Sabâhyâbhyantarah*' means
'existing both without and within.' 'Unborn' is 'not
born of anything,' *i.e.*, neither from itself nor from any
other, there being no other, from which it could be
born. As wind, etc., in the case of water bubbles etc., and
as the pot, etc., in the case of the different cavities of *âkás*,
so modifications of things, have birth for their source,
and all these modifications are denied when birth is
denied.   The drift is that ho is both without and within, unborn and therefore undecaying, immortal, change-

less, constant and fearless. Though he appears to be in the various bodies with *prána*, with mind, with senses and with their objects owing to the ignorance of those who perceive difference of conditions, such as bodies, etc., as they see in the *ákás* the colour etc., of the surface ; but still to those who see the reality, ho is without *prána,* etc. ; he is without *prána*, i.e., in whom the mind, which has various active powers and whose characteristic is motion, does not exist. He is without mind because in him the mind with its various powers of knowledge and with its characteristics of volition etc., does not exist. It should be understood that of him are denied the varieties of winds such as *prána*, the active sensory organs, their objects and accordingly intelligence, mind, the organs of knowledge and their objects. Accordingly, another Sruti says ' It seems to think and move.' He is *subhra* or pure, because both these conditions are thus denied of him. The *Akshara* which is beyond all, the *Avyákrita* whose nature is indicated as the seed condition of all name and form, as it is known to be the seed of all effects and causes ; '*param*,' because the *akshara* known as *avyákrita* is in its condition above all its modifications. The *Purusha* is beyond even this unmanifested *akshara*, i.e., not subject to any conditions. In whom is the *akshara* known as *ákás* with all the objects of duality strung together as warp and woof. How then could it be said to be without *prana*, etc ?. If *prána* etc., existed as such in their own forms before their creation like the *purusha*, then the *purusha* can be said to be with *prána* because of their then existence ; but they, the *prána* etc., do not, like the *purusha*, exist in their own forms, before their creation. So the highest *purusha* is without *prána* etc.

एतस्माज्जायते प्राणो मनः सर्वेन्द्रियाणि च ।
खं वायुर्ज्योतिरापः पृथिवी विश्वस्य धारिणी ॥ ३ ॥

From him are born the *prána*, the mind, all the sensory organs, the *ákás*, the wind, the fire, water and the earth which supports all.

Com.—As Devadatta is said to be ' *aputra* ' when a ' *putra*' is not born to him, so it is explained how it is said in this connection that in the case of the *purusha*, the *prána* etc., do not exist ; because from this *purusha* alone viewed as conditioned by the seed of name and form is born the *prána*, the modification of the object of ignorance, a mere name and in its nature a non-entity ; for another Sruti says 'The name is mere speech, a modification and a falsehood'; by *prána*, which is an object of ignorance and a falsehood, the highest cannot be said to be possessed of it (*prána*), as a sonless man cannot be said to have a son, by a son seen in dreams ; similarly the mind, all the sensory organs and their objects are born of this. Therefore that he is really without *prâna* etc., is established. It should be known that just as these *prâna* etc., did not really exist before the creation, so, even after absorption as the organs, the mind and the senses, so the *bhûtas* which are the causes of the bodies and objects. 'Kham,' the *âkâs*, the air internal and external, of various kinds such as *avaha*, etc. ; ' *Jotihi'*, fire. ' *Apah'*, water. ' *Prithivi'*, earth. ' *Visvasya*,' of all. All these whose attributes are sound, touch, form, taste and smell and which are respectively formed by the combination of the latter with the previous attributes are born of him. Having briefly stated the immortal, unconditioned, eternal *Purusha*, the object of *para vidya*, by the text ' Bright, formless etc,' the Sruti next proceeded to explain his nature in detail and at length. It is only when a thing is explained briefly and at length, it becomes capable of being easily understood as if explained by *Sûtras* and by their commentaries.

अग्निर्मूर्धा चक्षुषी चन्द्रसूर्यौ दिशः श्रोत्रे वागिवृताश्च वेदाः ।

वायुः प्राणो हृदयं विश्वमस्य पद्भ्यां पृथिवी ह्येष सर्वभूतान्तरात्मा

|| ४ ||

This is he the internal *âtman* of all created things whose head is *agni*, whose eyes are the sun, and the moon, whose ears are the . four directions, whose speeches are the emanated Vedas, whose breath is *váyu*, whose heart is all the universe and from whose feet the earth proceeded.

Com.—This text is intended to show that the *virát purusha* within the globe, who is born of *Hiranyagarbha* the first born, is born only and a modification, of this *purusha* though apparently distanced by an intermediate principle. The text also describes him. '*Agnihi*', the *deva loka* or *swarga*, from the Sruti .' This *loka* verily is *Agni*, O Gautama.' ' *Murdha*, ' head; whose eyes are the sun and the moon. The word ' *yasya*' (of whom) should be read in every clause. The word '*asya*' subsequently occurring being converted into ' *yasya*' whose speech are the opened, *i. e.*, celebrated Vedas. ' *Hridayam*,' heart. ' *Visvam*,' the whole universe. The whole universe is only a modification of the mind for it is absorbed into the mind during sleep and because it issues from the mind when waking, like sparks of fire and from whose feet the earth was born ; this deity, all-pervading, endless, the first embodied existence having for its body the three *lokas* is the interior *átman* of all created things ; for it is he who, in all created things, is the seer, the hearer, the thinker, the knower and who is the cause of all. It is next stated that all living beings who come into *samsara* through the five fires are also born of the same *purusha*.

तस्मादग्निः समिधो यस्य सूर्यः सोमात्पर्जन्य ओषधयः पृथिव्यां ।
पुमान्रेतः सिञ्चति योषितायां वह्वीः प्रजाः पुरुषात्संप्रसूताः ॥ ९ ॥

From him the *Agni* (*Dyu loka*) whose fuel is the sun ;
from the moon in the *dyu loka, parjanya* (clouds) ; from
the clouds, the medicinal plant that grows on earth ;
from these the male (fire) which sheds the semen on
woman, thus gradually many living beings such as
Brahmins etc. are born of the *Purusha.*

Com.—'From him', from the *Purusha.* '*Agni*', the
Dyuloka, a kind of abode for man. That Agni is described. '*Samidhah*', fuel ; for which the sun is, as it
were, a fuel ; for, it is by the sun that the *Dyu loka* is
lighted. From the moon emerging out of the *Dyu loka*,
parjanya, the second fire, is produced ; and from the
parjanya, the medicinal plants proceed, grow on earth ;
and from the medicinal plants offered to the *purusha*
fire serving as the material cause the man (fire) sheds
semen on the woman (fire). Thus gradually from the
purusha are produced many living beings such as Brahmins etc ; moreover the helps to *karma* and their fruits
also proceed from the Purusha.

तस्मादृचः साम यजूंषि दीक्षा यज्ञाश्च सर्वे क्रतवो दक्षिणाश्च ।
संवत्सरश्च यजमानश्च लोकाः सोमो यत्र पवते यत्र सूर्यः ॥ ६ ॥

From him the Rig, the Sama, the Yajur, *Diksha*,

sacrifices, all *Kratus*, *Dakshina*, the year, the sacrificer and the worlds which the moon sanctifies and the sun illuminates.

Com.—How ?. ' *Tasmát* ', from the *Purusha* ; ' *Richah* ', the *mantrás* whose letters, feet and endings are determined and which are marked by *Chhandas* (metre) like the *gáyatri*. Sáma with its fivefold and sevenfold classification characterized by *sthoka* and other *gita* (music). ' Yajus ', *mantras* in the form of sentences, whose letters, feet and endings are determined by no rules. Thus the threefold *mantras*. ' *Diksha* ', restrictions such as the wearing of a *mounjee* (a kind of cord) etc, imposed upon the performer (of a sacrifice). ' *Yajnás* ', all sacrifices such as *agnihotra* etc. ' *Kratu* ', sacrifices which require a *yúpa* (*i. e.*, sacrificial post). ' *Dakshinah* ', rewards distributed in sacrifice from a single cow up to un- bounded whole wealth. ' Year ', stated time as a neces- sary adjunct of *karma*. ' *Yajamána* ', the performer, *i. e.*, the sacrificer. The worlds which are the fruits of his *karma* are next described " which the moon renders sacred and where the sun shines "; these are attainable by the northern and southern routes and are the fruits of the *karma* performed by the knowing and the ignorant.

तस्माच् देवा बहुधा संप्रसूताः साध्या मनुष्याः पशवो वयांसि ।

17

प्राणापानौ व्रीहियवौ तपश्च श्रद्धा सत्यं ब्रह्मचर्यं विधिश्च ॥ ७ ॥

From him also the *devas* are variously born, the *sádhyas*, the men, the cattle, the bird, the *prána* and the *apána*, the corn and *yava*, *tapas*, devotion, truth, Brahmacharya and injunction.

Com.—Tasmát, 'from him also, from the *purusha*. 'Variously', in various groups such as *vasus* etc. *Samprasútah*, well born. *Sádhyas*, a species of Devas, *Men* those that are entitled to perform *karma* ; *Cattle*, both of the village and the forest. *Vayámsi*, birds. The food of men etc. The *Prána* and the *Apána* ; corn and *yava*, to be used for making *havis* (oblations). *Tapas*, both as an indispensable adjunct to *karma* whose efficacy lies in the purification of the performer and as an independent means of attaining the fruits of *karma*. *Devotion*, that state of mind which precedes the mental calm and a belief in a future state necessary to the accomplishment of all human ends. Similarly, truth *i. e.*, avoiding falsehood and speaking out what has really happened, without harm to others. *Brahmacharyam*, absence of sexual intercourse. *Injunction*, the statement of what ought to be done.

सप्त प्राणाः प्रभवन्ति तस्मात्सप्तार्चिषः समिधस्सप्तहोमाः ।
सप्त इमे लोका येषु चरन्ति प्राणा गुहाशया निहिताः सप्त सप्त ॥ ८ ॥

From him are born the seven *pránas*, the seven flames, their sevenfold fuel, the sevenfold oblation and these seven *lokas* where the *pránas* move, seven and seven in each living being lying in the cave, there fixed.

Com.—Again the seven *pránas*, *i. e.*, (organs of sense) in the head are born of this *purusha* alone. ' Their seven flames', their light which enlightens their objects. Similarly, the sevenfold fuel, their sevenfold objects; for, it is by these objects that the *pránas*, *i. c.*, organs of sense are fed. ' The sevenfold oblations', the perceptions of the sevenfold objects; for, another Sruti says : " He offers the oblation which consists in the perception of the objects by the senses." The seven *lokas*, *i. e.*, the seats of the senses where the *pránas* move. The clause " where the *pránas* move" is intended to exclude the vital airs, *i. e.*, *prána*, *apána* and the rest. 'Lying in the cave', lying during sleep in the body or the heart. 'Fixed', fixed by the creator. 'Seven and seven', in every living thing. The meaning of the context is that all *karma* performed by knowing men who propitiate their *atman* and the fruits of such *karma* as well as the *karma* performed by the ignorant and their means and fruits ; all these proceed only from the highest and the omniscient *purusha*.

अतः समुद्रा गिरयश्च सर्वेऽस्मात्स्यन्दन्ते सिन्धवः सर्वरूपाः ।

अतश्च सर्वा ओषधयो रसश्च येनैष भूतैस्तिष्ठते ह्यन्तरात्मा ॥९॥

From him proceed the oceans and all the mountains and the diverse rivers; from him also, all the medicinal plants and taste, by which encircled by the Bhûtas, *i.e.*, gross elements, the intermediate *átman*, *i.e.*, subtle body is seated.

Com.—'From him', from the *purusha*. 'The oceans', all, the salt ocean etc. 'Mountains', the Himalayas and the rest are all from this *purusha*. 'Syandante', flow. 'Rivers', such as the Ganges. 'Sarvarûpah', of many forms. From this *purusha* also proceed the medicinal plants such as corn, *yava*, paddy etc. 'Taste', sixfold such as sweetness etc. 'By which', by which taste· 'Bhûtaih', by the five gross *bhûtas*. 'Pariveshtitah', encircled. 'Tishthate', is seated. 'The internal *átman*', the subtle body so called because it is the *átman*, as it were, intermediate between the gross body and the soul proper.

पुरुष एवेदं विश्वं कर्म तपो ब्रह्म परामृतम् ।

एतद्यो वेद निहितं गुहायां सोऽविद्याग्रन्थिं विकिरतीह सोम्य ॥ १० ॥

The *purusha* alone is all this universe—Karma and Tapas. All this is Brahman, the highest and the immortal who knows this as seated in the cavity of the heart, unties the knot of ignorance even here, Oh good looking youth !

Com.—Thus, out of *purusha*, all this is born ; therefore as the Sruti says " Tho name is mere speech, a modification and a falsehood and the *purusha* alone is true." Therefore all this is only *purusha*. Tho universe has no separato existence apart from *purusha*. Henco to the question propounded " O Bhagavân, by knowing whom, all this becomes known," the answer has been given, *i. e.*, when this *purusha*, the supreme *âtman*, the first cause is known, it becomes clear that all this universe is *purusha* and nothing else exists except him. What then is this "all," it is thus explained. Karma is of the nature of Agnihotra and the rest. *Tapas*, knowledge and the fruit due to it. By ' all ' this much is meant. And all this is evolved out of Brahman. Therefore everything is Brahman. He who knows that he himself is this Brahman the highest and the immortal placed in the hearts of all living beings destroys tho denso tendencies of ignorance. *Iha*, even while living and not merely after death. *Soumya*, good looking.

————o————

Here ends the commentary
on the first part of the
Second Mundaka.

————o————

SECOND
Mundakopanishad.

---o---

PART II.

---o---

आविः सन्निहितं गुहाचरन्नाम महत्पदमत्रैतत्समर्पितम् ।
एजत्प्राणन्निमिषच्च यदेतज्ञानथ सदसद्वरेण्यं परं विज्ञानाद्यद्वरिष्ठं प्र-
जानाम् ॥ १ ॥

Bright, well-fixed, moving in the heart, great and the support of all; in him is all this universe centred, what moves, breathes and winks. Know this which is all that has form and all that is formless, which is to be sought after by all, which is beyond the reach of man's knowledge, and the highest of all.

· *Com.*—It is now explained how the *akshara* which is formless, could bo known. *Avihi*, bright, shining as the percipient of sound ctc., according to the Sruti, " It shines through its conditions of speech etc." It is seen in the heart of all living beings appearing there with the attributes of seeing, hearing, thinking, knowing etc. This Brahman shining is *Sannihita, i.e.,* well scated in the heart. It is celebrated as *guhácharan* because it moves in the cavity in modes of seeing, hearing etc. 'Great', because it is greater than all. *Padam*, reached by all, because it is the seat of all objects. How is it said to bo great eto?. Because in tho Brahman all this universe is centred as the various spokes aro in the wheel-ring of tho chariot. *Ejat*, moving, *i.e.*, birds etc; *prânet*, breathes, *i.e.*, men, cattle etc., having *prâna*, *apâna* etc; and 'winks', all that winks and all that winks *not*, from tho force of tho particle *cha*; this in which all is centred, know, O disciplo, that that is your own *âtman*; both *sat* and *asat*; for without it, *sat* and *asat*, that which has form and that which has not, *i. e.*, the gross and the subtle do not exist. *Varenyam*, covetable; because of all objects it is the only eternal entity. *Param*, distinct from, or, beyond; this is connected with the expression "knowledge of men" though remote; the meaning is that it is beyond the reach of worldly knowledge. *Varishtham*, the highest of all; because of all that is high, the Brahman is pre-eminently high, being free from all faults.

यदर्चिमद्यदणुभ्योऽणु च यस्मिँल्लोकाऽनिहिता लोकिनश्च ।
तदेतदक्षरं ब्रह्म स प्राणस्तदु वाङ्मनः । तदेतत्सत्यं तदमृतं त-
द्वेद्धव्यं सोम्य विद्धि ॥ २॥

What is bright, what is smaller than tho small, in what are centred all tho world and those that live in them is this immortal Brahman. That is *prána*, that is speech and mind. That is true and immortal; good looking youth. Strike thy mind upon that which should be struck by the mind.

Com.—Besides it is *archimat*, bright, because it is by the light of the Brahman that the sun etc. shine; again it is subtler than the subtlest (*i. e.*,) grain etc. From the particle *cha*, it is suggested that it is bigger than the biggest such as earth etc. In whom all the worlds such as earth etc., are fixed and men and the rest, inhabitants of those worlds; for all are well-known to depend upon " Intelligence", *i. e.*, Brahman; this immortal Brahman on which all depend is *prána*, speech, mind and all the instruments. It is their internal intelligence for the whole combination of *prána*, senses etc., is dependant upon that intelligence, according to the Sruti 'It is the *prána* of *prána* etc.' This immortal Brahman which is the internal intelligence of *prána* etc., is true and therefore endless. *Valdhavyam*, should be seized by the mind. The meaning is that the mind should be concentrated upon the Brahman. This being so, O good looking youth, strike that, *i. e.*, concentrate your mind upon that Brahman.

धनुर्गृहीत्वौपनिषदं महास्त्रं शरं ह्युपासानिशितं संधयीत ।

आयम्य तद्भावगतेन चेतसा लक्ष्यं तदेवाक्षरं साम्य विधि ॥२॥

Having taken the bow furnished by the Upanishads, the great weapon—and fixed in it the arrow rendered pointed by constant meditation and having drawn it with the mind fixed on the Brahman, hit, good looking youth! at that mark—the immortal Brahman.

Com.—How that is hit is now explained. *Dhanuh*, the bow. *Grihitvá*, having taken. *Upanishadam*, born in, *i. e.*, well-known in the Upanishads. *Mahástram*, great weapon, *i. e.*, the arrow; fix the arrow; of what quality is stated. *Upásánisilam*, rendered pointed by constant meditation, *i. e.*, purified; after fixing it and drawing it, *i. e.*, having drawn the mind and the senses from their external objects and bending, *i. e.*, concentrating them on the mark, for the bow here cannot be bent as by the hand; hit the mark—the immortal Brahman—above defined with thy mind, Oh good looking youth, engrossed by meditation upon the Brahman.

प्रणवो धनुः शरो ह्यात्मा ब्रह्म तल्लक्ष्यमुच्यते ।
अप्रमत्तेन वेद्धव्यं शरवत्तन्मयो भवेत् ॥ ४ ॥

The *Pranava* is the bow, the *Atman* is the arrow and the Brahman is said to be its mark. It should be hit by one who is self-collected and that which hits becomes, like the arrow, one with the mark, *i. e.*, Brahman.

18

Com.—What the bow and the rest above referred to are, is explained. The Pranava, *i. e.*, the syllable "Om" is the bow; as the bow is the cause of the arrow entering into the mark, so the syllable "Om" is the cause of the Atman entering into the Brahman ; for it is only when purified, by the repetition of *Pranava*, that the *Atman* supported by it becomes fixed in the Brahman without obstruction, as the arrow by the force of the bow is fixed in the mark. Therefore the *Pranava* is like a bow. The arrow is the *Paramâtman* itself conditioned as the *Atman* having entered the body here, as the sun enters the water, as the witness of all states of con- sciousness. That, like an arrow, is discharged towards itself—the immortal Brahman. Therefore the Brahman is said to be its mark, because it is seen to be the *Atman* itself by those who fix their mind upon it as on a mark. This being so, the Brahman which is the mark should be hit by one who is self-collected, *i. e.*, who is free from the excitement caused by a thirst to get at external objects, who is disgusted with every- thing, who has conquered his senses and whose mind is concentrated. When that is hit, the *Atman* becomes like the arrow, one with the mark, *i. e.*, the Brahman. Just as the success of the arrow is its becoming one with the mark, so the fruit here achieved is the *Atman* becoming one with the immortal Brahman by the dispelling of the notion that the body etc., is the *Atman*.

यस्मिन्द्यौः पृथिवी चान्तरिक्षमोतं मनः सह प्राणैश्च सर्वैः ।
तमेवैकं जानथ आत्मानमन्या वाचो विमुञ्चथामृतस्यैष सेतुः ॥९॥

He in whom the heaven, the earth, the *antariksha*
(sky), the mind with the *pranas* are centred; know
him to be the one *Atman* of all; abandon all other
speech; this is the road to immortality.

Com.—As the "Immortal" cannot be easily grasped
by the mind, the repetition is for the purpose of making
it more easily cognisable. He, the immortal Brahman,
in whom *Dyouh*, earth, and *antariksha* are centred as
also the mind with the other instruments; know him,
O disciples as "the one," the support of all; the *Atman*,
i. e., the internal principle of yourselves and all living
beings; having known that, leave off all other speech
of the nature of "Aparavidya" as also all Karma with
their aids elucidated by it; for, this, *i. e.*, the knowledge
of the Atman is the road to the attainment of emancipation, the bridge as it were by which the great ocean
of Samsara is crossed, as another Sruti says "having
known him thus, one travels beyond death; there is
no other road to emancipation."

अरा इव रथनाभौ संहता यत्र नाड्यः स एषोऽन्तश्चरते बहुधा जाय-
मानः ।

ओमित्येवं ध्यायथ आत्मानं स्वस्ति व: पराय तमस: परस्तात् ॥६॥

Where the nerves of the body meet together as the
spokes in the nave of a wheel, this Atman is within it
variously born ; meditate upon " Om " as the Atman.
May there be no obstacle to your going to the other
side beyond darkness.

Oom.—Within the heart where all nerves running
through the body meet together, as the spokes in the nave
of the wheel, this Atman, spoken of, dwells within, as the
witness of the states of consciousness, seeing, hearing,
thinking, knowing and as it were, being variously born
by the modifications of the mind such as anger, joy
etc; men in the world say 'He has *become* angry, he
has *become* joyful", according to the conditions of the
internal sense (mind); meditate upon Atman having
the syllable " Om " as your support and imagining as
stated. And it has been said " the preceptor who
knows must instruct the disciples." The disciples are
those who being desirous to acquire the knowledge of
the Brahman, have renounced Karma and taken the
road to emancipation. The preceptor gives his benedic-
tion that they may attain the Brahman without hindrance ; *svasti vah paráya*, let Him be without hindrance
to your reaching the other shore. *Parastát* ; beyond,
beyond what ? ; beyond the darkness of ignorance, *i.e.*,

for tho realisation of tho true nature of the Atman devoid of ignorance. He who should be reached after crossing the ocean of Samsâra and who is the subject of the Paravidya.

य: सर्वज्ञ: सर्वविदस्यैष महिमा भुवि दिव्येब्रह्मपुरे ह्येष व्योग्न्यात्मा प्रतिष्ठित: ।

मनोमय: प्राणशरीरनेता प्रतिष्ठितोऽन्ने हृदयं सन्निधाय तद्विज्ञानेन परिपश्यन्ति धीरा आनन्दरूपममृतं यद्विभाति ॥७॥

This Atman who knows all and all of every thing and whose glory is so celebrated on earth is seated in tho *âkâs* of the bright city of Brahman. He is conditioned by the mind, is the leader of the *prâna* and the body and is seated in food, *i. e.*, the body fixing the intelligence (in the cavity of their heart). The discerning people see by means of their superior knowledge on all sides the *âtman* which shines, all bliss and immortality.

Com.—Where He is, is now explained; the terms '*sarvajna*' and '*sarvavit*' have already been explained. He is again described; by the expression "whose glory is this" is meant "whose glory is celebrated". What is that glory? By whose commands stand supported the earth and the sky, by whose command, the sun and the moon always rotate as tho flaming fire-brand. By

whose command the rivers and the seas do not overstep
their limits, whose command all that is moveable and
immoveable likewise obey, whose commands in the
same way, tho seasons, the solstices, and the years do
not transgress; by whose commands all *karma*, their
performers and their fruits do not likewise go beyond
their appointed time; *that* is his glory. *Bhuvi*, in the
world. This Deva whose is all this glory and who is
omniscient. *Divye*, bright, *i. e.*, illuminated by all tho
states of consciousness. *Brahmapure*, in the lotus of
the heart, so called because the Brahman is always
manifesting himself there in the form of intelligence.
Vyomni, in the *ákás*, within the cavity of the heart.
He is perceived *as if* seated there; because otherwise
motion to or from, or fixity in a place is not possible for
him who is all-pervading like the *ákás*. *Manomaya*,
because seated in the heart, ho is perceived only by tho
modifications of the mind. (Thus) conditioned by the
mind. Leader of the *prána* and tho body, because he
leads the *prána* and the body from one gross body into another body. *Pratishthitah*, fixed. *Anne*, in the
food, *i. e.*, in the body which is a modification of the
food eaten and which grows and decays day by day.
Hridayam, intellect. *Sannidháya*, fixing—in tho cavity of tho lotus; for, the Atman is really seated in tho
heart and not in tho food. *Tat*, the entity of the

Atman. *Vijnánena*, by knowledge, thorough, produced by the teachings of the *sástras* and the preceptor and arising from control of the mind, control of the senses, meditation, complete renunciation and freedom from desire. *Paripasyanti*, see on all sides full. *Dhíráh*, the discerning. *Anandarúpam*, free·from all dangers, miseries and troubles. *Vibhúti*, shines much in oneself always.

भिद्यते हृदयग्रन्थिश्छिद्यन्ते सर्वसंशयाः ।

क्षीयन्ते चास्य कर्माणि तस्मिन्दृष्टे परावरे ॥ ८ ॥

When he that is both high and low is seen, the knot of the heart is untied; all doubts are solved; and all his *karma* is consumed.

Com.—The fruit of the knowledge of the Paramátman is stated to be the following. Loosened is "the knot of the heart", *i. e.*, the group of tendencies in the mind due to ignorance, the desire which clings to the intellect according to the Sruti "The desires which lie imbedded in the heart etc." This is attached to the heart (intellect) not to the Atman. *Bhidyate*, undergoes destruction; doubts regarding all knowable things have their solution—doubts which perplex worldly men up to their death, being (continuous) like the stream of the Ganges; of the man whose doubts have been solved and whose ignorance has been dispelled, such *karma* as was anterior to the birth of knowledge in this life, such as was performed by him in previous births and had not begun to bear fruit and such as was existing at the birth of knowledge come to an end; but *not* that *karma* which brought about *this* birth, for it had begun to bear fruit. He, " the omniscient", not subject to *samsâra*; ' both high and low', high as being the cause and low as being the effect; when he is seen directly as " I am he", one attains emancipation, the cause of *samsâra* being uprooted.

हिरण्मये परे कोशे विरजं ब्रह्म निष्कलम् ।
तच्छुभ्रं ज्योतिषां ज्योतिस्तदात्मविदो विदुः ॥ ९ ॥

The stainless indivisible Brahman, the pure, the light of all lights is in the innermost sheath of golden hue. That is what the knowers of the Atman know.

Oom.—The three following texts briefly elucidate the meaning already expressed. *Hiranmaya*, golden, *i.e.*, full of light, or, bright with intelligence and knowledge. ' The highest sheath', sheath, as it were, of a sword ; *highest*, because it is the place where " the Atman is realised as located" and because it is the innermost of all. *Virajam*, free from the taint of ignorance and all other faults. *Brahma*, because it is the greatest of all and Atman of all. *Nishkalam*, that from which the *kalâs* had proceeded, *i.e.*, devoid of parts ; because it is untainted and devoid of parts, therefore it is *subhram* or pure. The light of all lights, whose light enlightens even those that illumine all other things such as fire etc. The meaning is that the brightness of even the fire, etc. is due to the splendour of the intelligence of the Brahman within; the light of the Atman is the highest light which is not illumined by other lights. 'The knowers of the *atman*', those 'discerning' men who know the Self as the witness of the objective states of consciousness regarding sound and the rest; as it is the highest light, it is only those who follow (are in) the subjective state of consciousness, not others, who follow (are in) the perceptions of external objects, that know it.

न तत्र सूर्यो भाति न चन्द्रतारकं नेमा विद्युतो भान्ति कुतोऽयमग्निः ।
तमेव भान्तमनुभाति सर्वं तस्य भासा सर्वमिदं विभाति ॥१०॥

The sun shines not there; nor the moon and the stars. Nor do these lightnings shine. How could this fire? All shine after him who shines. All this is illumined by his radiance.

Com.—How that is the light of all lights is explained. The sun though enlightening all, does not shine in, *i.e.*, does not illumine the Brahman which is his Atman; for, the sun illumines the whole universe other than the Atman with the light of the Brahman, but

19

has not in himself the capacity to illuminate. Similarly neither the moon and the stars nor the lightning shines. How could this fire which is in the range of our vision ?. Why dilate ?. This universe which shines, shines with the light of him, the lord of all, who shines being himself luminosity. Just as water and the rest by their contact with fire, heat with the heat of the fire, but not by their own inherent power, so all this universe, the sun and the rest shine with the light of the Brahman. As it is the Brahman alone that thus shines and shines with varying light in its diverse manifestations, itself luminosity, is inferred ; for, that which is not itself light cannot illumine others as we see that pots, etc., do not illumine others and that the. sun and the rest having light, illumine others.

ब्रह्मैवेदमग्रृतं पुरस्ताह्रस पधाह्रस दक्षिणताधोत्तरेण ।
अधधोर्च्वं च प्रसृतं ब्रह्मैवेदं विश्वमिदं वरिष्ठं ॥ ११ ॥

All-this before is immortal Brahman ; certainly all
· behind is Brahman ; all to the south and to the north ;
all below and all alone stretched out, i.e. extended, all
this is certainly Brahman, the highest. ·

Com.—The statement, Brahman alone the light of
lights is true and that all else is only its modification,
a matter of speech is a mere name and falsehood first
made and logically demonstrated at length (after-

wards) is affirmed again as a conclusion by this *mantra*. That which is before us and which, in the eyes of the ignorant, appears to be not Brahman is certainly Brahman. Similarly what is behind us; so, that to the south ; so, that to the north : so, that below, and that above and all that is extended everywhere in the form of effect, appearing otherwise than Brahman and possessed of name and form. Why say much ?. All this vast universe is Brahman certainly· All perception otherwise than as Brahman is mere ignorance, just as the perception of a serpent in a robe. The declaration of the Vedas is that the one Brahman alone is really true.

———o———

Here ends the second part of the second Mundaka.

———o———

THIRD
𝕸𝖚𝖓𝖉𝖆𝖐𝖔𝖕𝖆𝖓𝖎𝖘𝖍𝖆𝖉.

---o---

PART I.

---o---

द्वा सुपर्णा सयुजा सखाया समानं वृक्षं परिषस्वजाते ।
तयोरन्यः पिप्पलं स्वाद्वत्त्यनश्रन्नन्यो अभिचाकशीति ॥ १ ॥

Two inseparable companions of fine plumage perch
on the self-same tree. One of the two feeds on the
delicious fruit. The other not tasting of it looks on.

Com.—The Paravidya has been explained by
which the immortal 'Purusha' or the Truth could be
known, by whose knowledge the cause of *samsara*,
such as the knot of the heart etc. can be totally destroyed. Yoga which is the means to the realization
of the Brahman has also been explained by an illustration "taking the bow and the rest". Now the
subsequent portion is intended to inculcate the auxiliary helps to that *yoga*, as truth etc. Chiefly the
truth is here determined by another mode as it is extremely difficult to realize it. Here, though already
done, a *mantra* (brief) as an aphorism is introduced

for tho purpose of ascertaining the absolute entity. *Suparnau*, two of good motion or two birds ; (the word "Suparna" being used to denote birds generally) ; *Sayujau*, inseparable, constant, companions ; *Sakhayau*, bearing the same name or having the same cause of manifestation. Being thus, they are perched on the same tree ('same', because the place where they could be perceived is identical). 'Tree' here means 'body' ; because of the similitude in their liability to be cut or destroyed. *Parishasvajâte*, embraced ; just as birds go to the same tree for tasting the fruits. This tree as is well known has its root high up (i.e., in Brahman) and its branches (*prâna* etc.) downwards; it is transitory and has its source in *Avyakta (mâya)*. It is named 'Kshetra' and in it hang the fruits of the *karma* of all living things. It is here that the Atman conditioned in the subtle body to which ignorance, desire, *karma* and their unmanifested tendencies cling and Isvara are perched like birds. Of these two so perched, one, i. e., *kshetrajna* occupying the subtle body eats, i.e., tastes from ignorance the fruits of *karma* marked as happiness and misery, palatable in many, and diversified modes; the other, i. e., the lord, eternal, pure, intelligent and free in his nature, omniscient and conditioned by *mâya* does not eat ; for, he is the director of both the eater and the thing eaten, by the fact of his mere existence as the eternal witness (of all); not tasting, he merely looks on; for his mere *witnessing* is *direction* as in the case of a king.

समाने वृक्षे पुरुषो निमग्नोऽनीशाया शोचति मुह्यमानः ।
जुष्टं यदा पश्यत्यन्यमीशामस्य महिमानमिति वीतशोकः ॥ २ ॥

On the self same tree the *Jiva* drowned as it were and perplexed, grieves owing to helplessness. But when he sees the other, the lord who is worshipped by all and his glory, he becomes absolved from grief.

Com.—In this state of things the *Jiva*, *i.e.*, the enjoyer occupying the body as above described under the heavy load of ignorance, desire and thirst for the fruits of Karma etc, sinks down like a bottle-gourd in the waters of the sea, is convinced beyond doubt that the body is the *átman* and thinking that he is the son of this man or the great-grandson of that, lean or stout, with or without good qualities, is enjoying or suffering, and that there is none but him, is born, dies, is united with and parted from relations and kinsmen; therefore he grieves from helplessness thus: "I am good for nothing I have lost my son, my wife is dead, what avails my life" and so forth and is subject to anxiety from ignorance owing to numerous kinds of troubles; but when thus constantly degenerating in births, of *pretas*, beasts, men and the like, he happens, owing to the result of pure deeds stored up in many (previous) births to be instructed in the path of Yoga by some preceptor surpassingly compassionate and being qualified by abstinence from giving pain, truth speaking, continence, complete renunciation and control over the internal and external senses and with his mind concentrated, finds by dint of meditation, the other who is approached by different paths of Yoga and by the followers of Karma distinct from him, conditioned in the body, not subject to the bondage of Samsara, unaffected by hunger, thirst, grief, ignorance, decay and death and lord over all the universe and thinks thus: "I am the *âtman*, alike in all, seated in every living thing and not the other the illusory *âtman*, enclosed under conditions created by ignorance and this glory—this universe is mine, the lord of all," then he becomes absolved from grief, *i. e.*, is released entirely from the ocean of grief, *i. e.*, his object is accomplished.

यदा पश्यः पश्यते रुक्मवर्णं कर्तारमीशं पुरुषं ब्रह्मयोनिम् ।
तदा विद्वान्पुण्यपापे विधूय निरञ्जनः परमं साम्यमुपैति ॥ ३ ॥

When the seer sees him of golden hue, the creator, lord, Purusha and the source of (Apara) Brahma, then the knower, having shaken off all deeds of merit and sin, attains supremo equality, being untouched with stain.

Com.—Another *mantra* also convoys the same meaning at length. *Yala*, when; *Pasyaha*, one who sees, *i. e.*, a learned man, *i. e.*, a man of practice. *Rukma-varnam*, of self-resplendent nature, or, of imperishable brightness as that of gold. 'Creator,' of all the universe; *Brahmayonim*, the Brahman who is the source of the manifested Brahman. When he sees the Brahman thus, then the learned man shaking off, or burning away good and bad deeds, forming a bondage to their root and being unaffected, i. e., freed from grief, attains that supreme equality which is identity with the Brahman. The equality in matters involving duality is certainly inferior to this.

प्राणो ह्येष यः सर्वभूतैर्विभाति विजानन्विद्वान्भवते नातिवादी ।
आत्मक्रीड आत्मरतिः. क्रियावानेष ब्रह्मविदां वरिष्ठः ॥ ४ ॥ .

This is indeed Prâna, *i. e.*, Isvara, shining variously with all living beings. Knowing him, the wise man becomes not a talker regarding anything olse. Sporting in self, delighted in self and, doing acts (enjoined), this man is the best of those who know the Brahman.

Com.—Again this Isvara is the *prâna* of *prâna*. *This*, now treated of. 'All living things,' from the Brahman down to the worm. The instrumental case

in "*Sarvabhútaih*" has the force of "thus become."
The meaning is 'existing in all living things, *i.e.*, the
átman of all.' *Vibháti*, shines variously. The man of
knowledge who directly realizes Him who is in all
things as his own Atman and thinks "I am he" does
not become an *atirádin*, merely by the knowledge of
the import of the *mahárákya*. *Ativádi*, means one
whose nature is to talk of all other things more, when
he sees that all is the Atman and nothing else exists;
how then could he talk of anything else. It is only
where one sees anything else, he could well talk of
that; but this man of knowledge sees, hears and knows
none other than the Atman; so he is not a talker of
anything else. Again, he is an *átmakrídah*, *i. e.*, one
whose sport is within his own Atman and not elsewhere
such as son, wife, etc. Similarly he is *átmaratih*, *i.e.*,
one who delights or revels in his own Atman. The term
krídá or play requires some external help. But delight
or revelling does not require any external help but
indicates merely the attachment to an external object.
This is the distinction. Similarly, *kriyáván*, i. e.,
one whose activity consists in knowledge, meditation,
freedom from desire, etc. But if the reading be
"*átmaratikriyáván*" (a compound) the meaning is he
whose activity is mere delight in man; as between the
Bahuvrihi and the "*matup*" ending, one is sufficient

20

without the other; but some contend that the single compound, denotes a combination of both *karma* i. e., Agnihotra and the rest, and the knowledge of Brahman. " It is not possible for one to be playing with external objects and at the same time to be delighted in self. It is only the man who has turned away from external activity that becomes delighted in self; for, external activity and delight in itself are opposed to each other ; for, it is not possible that darkness and light could exist in the same place. Therefore the statement that a combination of Karma and knowledge is inculcated by this text is certainly the prattle of the ignorant. This also follows from the Srutis " Leave off from all other speech " and " by reuunciation of Karma etc. " Therefore he alone is " *Kriyâvân* " whose activity consists in knowledge, meditation etc., and who is a Sanyasin not transgressing the limits of prohibitory injunctions. Such a man as is not an *ativâdin*, as sports in his own self, as delights in himself and · as is a Kriyâvân (whose activity is aforesaid) is the first among all the knowers of Brahman.

सत्येन लभ्यस्तपसा ह्येष आत्मा सम्यग्ज्ञानेन ब्रह्मचर्येण नित्यम् ।
अन्तःशरीरे ज्योतिर्मयो हि शुभ्रो यं पश्यन्ति यतयः क्षीणदोषाः ॥९॥

This Atman within the body, resplendent and pure, can be reached by truth and *tapas*, by sound know-

ledge and by abstinence from sexual pleasures constantly
practised ; he is within the body, resplendent and pure;
him, assiduous Sanyasins see, their faults removed.

Com.—Now truth and the rest chiefly characterized
by restraint are enjoined upon a *bhikshu*, *i.e.*, mendicant,
as auxiliary aids with sound knowledge ; he should be
attained by truth, *i.e.*, by abstaining from falsehood; as
also by *tapas*, *i.e.*, by concentration of the senses and
the mind, which is declared to be the highest *tapas*;
for, it is this which is of greatest help as it is turned
towards beholding the Atman, not the other forms of
tapas, such as the performance of the *chándráyana* (a
penance), etc. " This Atman should be attained"
should be read into every clause. 'By good knowledge ',
by beholding the Atman as it really is. 'By *brahmacharya* ', by abstinence from sexual pleasure. *Nityam*,
always. The word " always " should be read with every
one of the words ' truth,' ' *tapas*,' etc. Just as a lamp
within a building illumines every part of it, it will be
said later on that they see the Atman in whom there
is neither deceit, nor falsehood, nor cunning. Who this
Atman is that should be attained by these aids is explained. ' Within the body ', in the midst of the body,
i.e., in the *ákás* of the lotus of the heart. 'Resplendent',
of golden hue. *Subhra*, pure. The· *yatayah*, *i. e.*,
those who are habitually seeking, *i.e.*, the Sanyasins,

'their faults removed', i.e., devoid of all taint of mind such as anger etc., find this *âtman.* Tho drift is that the *âtman* is attained by Sauyasins with these aids as truth, etc., constantly practised and cannot be attained by them occasionally practised. This text is a eulogy of such aids as truth etc.

सत्यमेव जयति नानृतं सत्येन पन्था विततो देवयानः ।
येनाक्रमन्त्यृषयो ह्याप्तकामा यत्र तत्सत्यस्य परमं निधानम् ॥६॥

Truth alone wins, not falsehood; by truth, tho Devayânah (tho path of the Devas) is widened, that by which the seers travel on, having nothing to wish for, to where there is that—the highest treasure attained by truth.

Com.—Truth alone, *i. e.*, he who speaks the truth alone, wins; not he who utters falsehood, for thero can be neither victory nor defeat between abstract truth and falsehood where they do not cling to men. It is well known in tho world that he who utters falsehood is defeated by him who speaks the truth; not the converse. Therefore it is established that truth is a strong auxiliary; again tho superiority of truth as an aid is also known from tho *sastras;* how?. It is only by truth, *i.e.*, by a determination to speak what had occurred, tho road named "Dovayânah" (the way of tho gods) is widened; *i. e.*, is kept up continually; by which road,

seers free from deceit, delusion, fraud, pride, vanity
and falsehood and having no desires, go about to where
the absolute truth, the highest treasure covetable by
man and attainable by the important aid, truth, exists.
The expression "where the greatest etc" is connected
with the preceding clause "the road by which they
go is widened by truth." What that is and what its
characteristics are will be explained.

बृहच्च तद्दिव्यमचिन्त्यरूपं सूक्ष्माच्च तत्सूक्ष्मतरं विभाति ।
दूरात्सुदूरे तदिहान्तिके च पश्यत्स्विहैव निहितं गुहायाम् ॥ ७ ॥

That shines as vast, heavenly, of unthinkable form
and subtler than the subtle, much farther than the distant, near, also here, and seen fixed in the cavity, by
the intelligent.

Com.—The *Brahman* now treated of and attainable
by truth, etc., is vast, because it is all-pervading;
'heavenly,' self-luminous and imperceivable by the
senses. Therefore alone is it that its form is unthinkable; it is subtler than even the subtle, such as the
ákás and the rest; for, being the cause of all, it is of
unsurpassing subtlety. *Vibháti*, shines diversely, *i.e.*,
in various forms such as that of the sun, the moon etc.
Again it is farther, even from the most distant places;
for, the Brahman cannot be in the least approached by
the ignorant. It is also near, *i. e.*, in the body itself;

because it is the *âtman* of those who know and because it is within all, from the Sruti which declares
it to be even within the *âkás.* 'In those who see',
among the intelligent men. 'Fixed', seated, *i. c.*, seen
by *yogis*, as possessed of the activity of seeing etc.
Where ? ; in the cavity, *i. e.*, in the intellect ; for it is
seen as lodged there by those who know ; still, though
lodged there, it is not seen by the ignorant, as it is
veiled by ignorance.

न चक्षुषा गृह्यते· नापि वाचा नान्यैर्देवैस्तपसा कर्मेणा वा ।
ज्ञानप्रसादेन विशुद्धसत्त्वस्ततस्तु तं पश्यते निष्कलं ध्यायमानः ॥८॥

Ho is not grasped by the eye ; nor by speech ; nor
by other senses ; nor by *tapas* ; nor by *karma* ; when
one's mind is purified by the clearness of knowledge,
then alone he sees the indivisible (Brahman) by contemplation.

Com.—Again, a special aid to the attainment of
Brahman is explained. It is not seen by the eye of
anybody, because it has no form ; nor is it grasped by
speech, because it cannot be the subject of words ; nor
by the other senses. Though *tapas* is an aid to the
attainment of all, the Brahman cannot be reached by
karma enjoined by the Vedas, such as *agnihotra* and
the rest though their greatness is well known. What
then is the means by which it could be grasped is

explained. *Gnâna prasâdena*, though the intellect in all men is by nature competent to know the Atman, still being polluted by such faults, as love for external objects etc., and hence unclear and impure, it does not, like a stained mirror and muddy water, grasp the entity of the Atman though always near; but when, by removal of the polluting taint, such as desire etc., produced by contact with the objects of the senses, it is made clear and calm like mirror and water, then the intellect becomes clear; by this clearness of the intellect the mind is purified and the man becomes competent to realize the Brahman. Therefore he sees the Atman which has no parts, by meditation, having recourse to such helps such as truth etc., having controlled his senses and with a concentrated mind.

एषोऽणुरात्मा चेतसा वेदितव्यो यस्मिन्प्राण: पञ्चधा संविवेश ।
प्राणैश्चित्तं सर्वमोतं प्रजानां यस्मिन्विशुद्धे विभवत्येष आत्मा ॥९॥

This subtle Atman should be known by the mind as being in the body, whose *prâna* entered in five different forms; the mind in all creatures is pervaded by these *prânas*. When it is purified, then the Atman shines out of itself.

Com.—This Atman, who is thus seen, is subtle and should be known by the mind, *i.e.*, by the mere intellect purified. Where is this *Atman?*; in the body which, *prâna*

in five different forms, has well entered. The meaning
is: he should be known by the mind as existing in the
body, i.e., in the heart; by mind, how circumstanced
should he be known, is explained; mind in all creatures is pervaded by the *prânâs* and the senses, as
milk by oil, and fuel by fire. The mind in all living
beings is well known in the world, to be possessed of
intelligence; when the mind is purified, i. e., freed
from the taint of grief etc., then this Atman above-
defined shines out, shows itself out, by itself.

यं यं लोकं मनसा संविभाति विशुद्धसत्त्वः कामयते यांश्च कामान् ।
तं तं लोकं जयते तांश्च कामांस्तस्मादात्मज्ञं ह्यर्चयेद्भूतिकामः ॥ १ ०॥

Whatever worlds he covets by his mind, and whatever objects he wishes for the man of pure mind, he gains
those worlds and those objects ; therefore, let him who
longs for *Bhûti* (manifested power) worship him who
knows the *âtman*.

Com.—This text explains that the man who identi-
fies the *âtman* of all with his own, obtains as the fruits
thereof, all that he longs for ; because of the fact that
he is the *Atman* of all. Whatever worlds, i.e., such as
those of the *manes* and the rest, he covets either himself,
or for others, or whatever enjoyments he wishes for the
man of pure mind who is free from all grief and who
knows the *âtman*, he obtains those worlds and those en-

joyments. Therefore, *i.e.*, because the wishes of the knower of the *Atman* are always realised; let one who longs for *vibhûtis* propitiate the knower of the Atman whose mind is purified by such knowledge, by cleaning his feet with water, personal service, prostration and the rest; therefore, ho is worthy of worship.

———o———

Here ends the first part of
the Third Mundaka.

———o———

THIRD
Mundakopanishad.

———o———

———o———

स वेदैतत्परमं ब्रह्म धाम यत्र विश्वं निहितं भाति शुभ्रम् ।
उपासते पुरुषं ये ह्यकामास्ते शुक्रमेतदतिवर्तन्ति धीराः ॥ १ ॥

He knows the highest Brahman, the place where all
this universe rests, and which shines with clear brightness. The intelligent, who, free from all desire, worship
this man, travel beyond this seed.

Com.—As he knows the Brahman above defined, the
highest of all, the place where all desires rest, where
all the universe rests and which shines purely by its
own light, the intelligent, who free from yearning for
vibhûti and with a desire for emancipation worship
even this man as the highest, travel beyond this seed,
i.e., the material cause of embodied existence, *i.e.,* are
never born again of the womb, according to the

Sruti, 'He does not like any abode.' The meaning
is that one should worship such a knower.

कागान्य: कामयते मन्यमानः स कामभिर्जायते तत्र तत्र ।

पर्याप्तकामस्य कृतात्मनस्त्विहैव सर्वे प्रविलीयन्ति कामाः ॥ २ ॥

He, who broods on and longs for objects of desire, is
born there and there with such desires; but of him
whose desires havo been fulfilled and who has realised,
the Atman, tho desires end even here (in this world).

Com.—This text shows that tho primary help to
him who is desirous of emancipation is the renunciation of all desire. He who covets visible or invisible
objects of desire, brooding on their virtues is born
again and again with those desires of external objects
which are incentive to the performance of good and bad
deeds. Wherever his desires direct him to perform
karma for the realisation of their objects, he is born
with those self-same desires in those objects. But of
him who from a sound knowledge of the absolute truth
has all his desires fulfilled, because the Atman is the
object of his desire and whose Atman through knowledge
has been made to assume its highest, *i.e.,* true form by
the removal of the lower form imposed on it by ignorance, all desires impelling him to do meritorious and
sinful deeds are destroyed even while his body lasts.

The drift is that desires do not spring up, because the causes of their rising are destroyed.

नायमात्मा प्रवचनेन लभ्यो न मेधया न वहुना श्रुतेन ।
यमेवैप‧वृणुते तेन लभ्यस्तस्यैष आत्मा विवृणुते तनुं स्वाम् ॥३॥

This Atman cannot be attained by dint of study or intelligence or much hearing—whom ho wishes to attain—by that it can be attained. To him this Atman reveals its true nature.

Com.—If thus the realisation of tho *âtman* is the greatest gain of all, it may be thought that means such as study etc. should be largely employed for its attainment. This text is intended to dispel that notion. This *âtman* which has been explained and whose realisation is the highest object of human desire cannot be attained by means of much study of tho Vedas and the Sastras. Similarly not by intelligence, *i. e.*, by a retentive memory of tho purport of writings; nor by much heard, *i. e.*, by much hearing. By what then could the *Atman* be attained is explained. The *Paramâtman* whom this knower wishes to attain, by that seeking alone can that Brahman be attained; not by any other means, because his nature is always attained. What is the nature of this knower's attainment of the *Atman* is explained. As pot etc. reveals his form where there is light, so does the Atman concealed by ignorance reveal his true nature when there is knowledge. The drift is the wish for the realisation of the *Atman* after renouncing all others is alone the means to the attainment of the *Atman*.

नायमात्मा बलहीनेन लभ्यो न च प्रमादात्तपसो वाप्यलिङ्गात् ।
एतैरुपायैर्यतते यस्तु विद्वास्तस्येन आत्मा विशते ब्रह्मधाम ॥ ४ ॥

This *Atman* cannot be attained by one devoid of strength or by excitement or by *tapas* devoid of *linga*. But of the knower who strives with these aids, the *Atman* enters into the Brahman.

Com.—Combined with the wish to realise the *Atman*, strength, absence of excitement, and knowledge coupled with *Sanyása* are helps; because this *Atman* cannot be attained by one devoid of strength produced by concentration on the *Atman* or by excitement caused by associating with objects of the world, as son, cattle and the rest, or by *tapas* devoid of *linga*. '*Tapas*' here means 'knowledge'. "*Linga*" means "Sanyása". The meaning is that the *Atman* cannot be attained by knowledge without *Sanyása*. But of the knower who, with these aids, strength, absence of excitement, *sanyása* and knowledge—strives intent after the *Atman*, the Atman enters its abode, the Brahman.

संप्राप्यैनमृषयो ज्ञानतृप्ताः कृतात्मानो वीतरागाः प्रशान्ताः ।
ते सर्वगं सर्वतः प्राप्यधीरा युक्तात्मानः सर्वमेवाविशन्ति ॥ ५ ॥

Having attained Him, the seers content with their
knowledge, their purpose accomplished, free from all
desire, and with full composure, having attained the
all-pervading Atman on all sides, ever concentrated in
their minds, enter into everything.

Com.—How they enter into Brahman is explained.
Having known him well, the seers content with that
Knowledge and not by any external means of delight
tending to the growth of their body, their *Atman* having
become one with the *Paramâtman*, free from the fault of
desire etc., their senses subdued, having attained him
all-pervading like the *âkâs* on all sides, i.e., not in any
particular place limited by conditions (what then do
they attain ? The Brahman itself, one and without a
second as their own Atman), being discerning and with
concentrated minds enter into everything when their
body falls, i. c., cast off all limitations imposed by
ignorance as the *âkâs* in the pot when the pot is broken.
Thus do the Knowers of Brahman enter into Brahman
abode.

वेदान्तविज्ञानसुनिश्चितार्थाः सन्यासयोगाद्यतयः शुद्धसत्त्वाः ।
ते ब्रह्मलोकेषु परान्तकाले परामृताः परिमुच्यन्ति सर्वे ॥ ६ ॥

Having without doubt well ascertained the significance of the knowledge of Vedânta, the seekers their
minds purified by dint of renunciation, attain the
worlds of the Brahman and when their body falls, their
Atman being one with the highest immortal Brahman,
are absolved all round.

   Com.—Having without doubt determined the object of
the knowledge of Vedânta, *i.e.*, that Brahman should be
known, the seekers, their minds purified by dint of
renunciation of all *karma* and by being centred in the
pure Brahman, attain the worlds of the Brahman at the
end of *samsâra* which for the seekers after emancipation
corresponds to the time of death of those rotating in
samsâra. As men who seek emancipation are many,
the world of Brahman, though one, appears to be many
or is reached as many; so the plural number 'worlds of
the Brahman' is used. Brahman being the world
reached, the expression 'in the worlds of the Brahman'
means 'in Brahman.' *Pârâmritâh*, they whose *âtman*
has become the highest immortal, *i.e.*, Brahman. They
become the highest and immortal Brahman even during
life and are absolved in all sides like a lamp that has
gone out and like the *âkás* in the pot, *i.e.*, they have
no need of any other place to go to; for the *Sruti* and
the *Smriti* say " as the footmark of birds in the air and
that of aquatic animals in water are not seen, so the

track of the knowing men" and they go by no road, who would reach the ends of the roads of *samsára*. Motion limited by place is only in *samsára*, because it is accomplished by means limited; but as the Brahman is all, it cannot be reached in a limited space; if the Brahman were limited in respect of place, it would like a substance having form, have a beginning and an end, be dependent on another, composed of parts, non-eternal and be a product. But the Brahman cannot be like that; so its attainment too cannot be limited by conditions of place.

गताः कलाः पञ्चदश प्रतिष्ठा देवाश्च सर्वे प्रतिदेवतासु ।

कर्माणि विज्ञानमयश्च आत्मा परेऽव्यये सर्वे एकीभवन्ति ॥ ७ ॥

The fifteen *kalás* go back to their source; all the powers seated on the senses go back to their corresponding deities and all his *karma* and the *átman*, all these become one, in the highest and imperishable Brahman.

Com.—Moreover, the knowers of Brahman regard emancipation as consisting only in the release from bondage, *samsára*, ignorance and the rest not as something produced. Besides at the time of emancipation the *kalás* which produce the body, *pránás* etc., go back to their own seat, *i.e.*, cause. The word '*Pratishthá*' is

22

accusative plural. Fifteen : fifteen in number already enumerated in the last *prasna* and well-known. *Devas*, the powers adhering to the body, and lodged in the senses such as the eye etc. ; all these go to the corresponding deities such as the sun etc.; also those actions of the seeker after emancipation which have not begun to bear fruit (for those which have begun to bear fruit can be consumed only by enjoyment) and the *Atman* limited by the intellect, *i. e.*, who, mistaking the condition of the intellect so caused by ignorance for the *Atman*, has here entered into various bodies like the image of the sun etc. into water etc. (Karma being intended for the benefit of the *Atman*). Therefore ' *Vijnánamaya* ' means ' chiefly possessed of intellect.' These and the *Vijnánamaya* Atman, after removal of the conditions imposed, become mingled as one in the Brahman, the highest, the imperishable, endless, indestructible, all-pervading like the *ákás*, unborn, undecaying, immortal, beneficent, fearless, having neither before or after, nor in, nor out, without a second, unconditioned, lose their distinctive features, *i. e.*, become one as the images of the sun etc. become one with the sun when the surface, such as water (in which he is reflected) is withdrawn and as the *ákás* within the pot etc. becomes one with the *ákás* when the pot etc. is withdrawn.

यथा नद्यः स्यन्दमानाः समुद्रेऽस्तं गच्छन्ति नामरूपे विहाय ।
तथा विद्वान्नामरूपाद्विमुक्तः परात्परं पुरुषमुपैति दिव्यम् ॥ ८ ॥

Just as rivers flowing become lost in an ocean, giving both their name and form, just so, the knower, freed from name and form, attains the bright *purusha* which is beyond the *avyakta*.

Com.—Moreover, just as flowing streams such as the Ganges and the rest having reached the sea give up their distinct individuality in it, losing both their names and form, so, the knower being freed from name and form, created by ignorance, reaches the resplendent *purusha* above defined, who is beyond the *avyakta* already explained

स यो ह वै तत्परमं ब्रह्म वेद ब्रह्मैव भवति नास्याब्रह्मवित्कुले भवति ।
तरति शोकं तरति पाप्मानं गुहाग्रन्थिभ्यो विमुक्तोऽमृतो भवति ॥९॥

He who knows that highest Brahman becomes even Brahman; and in his line, none who knows not the Brahman will be born. He crosses grief and virtue and vice and being freed from the knot of the heart, becomes immortal.

Com.—It may be said that numerous obstacles are well known to exist in the attainment of good and that even the knower of Brahman may therefore be

impeded either by some grief or other, or he made to
take some other course by some other being such as
the Devas, reach some other after death and not reach
Brahman. This cannot be; for all obstacles have
already been removed by knowledge. Emancipation
knows only the obstacle of ignorance and no other
obstacle; because it is eternal and is being the Atman
itself. Therefore, he in the world who knows that
highest Brahman, as " I am directly that" does not
take any other course. It is impossible even for the
devás to throw any obstacle in his attempt to reach the
Brahman, because he becomes the Atman of all these;
therefore he who knows the Brahman becomes even
Brahman. Moreover in the line of this knower, there
will not be born any who knows not the Brahman;
again he overcomes even during life the heart-burning
caused by frustration of his many desires, crosses over
karma known as vice and virtue and being freed from
"the knots of the heart" caused by ignorance, becomes
immortal. It has already been said " the knot of the
heart is untied, etc."

तदेतदृचाऽभ्युक्तं । क्रियावन्तः श्रोत्रिया ब्रह्मनिष्ठाः स्वयं जुह्वत ए-
कर्षि श्रद्धयन्तः ।
तेषामेवैतां ब्रह्मविद्यां वदेत शिरोव्रतं विधिवद्यैस्तु चीर्णम् ॥१०॥

This is explained by the *mantra* "who perform the *karma* enjoined, who are *srotriyas*, who are centred in the Brahman (lower) and who with faith, offer oblations themselves to the fire named *Ekarshi*, perform the vow named *Sirovrata* (who duly carry a fire on the head); to those alone, let one teach this knowledge of the Brahman."

Com.—Now, the Upanishad concludes by indicating the rule regarding the teaching of the knowledge of Brahman. This, the rule about the teaching of the knowledge of Brahman is expounded by this text. Who perform the *karma* enjoined, who are Srotriyas, who being engaged in the worship of the manifested Brahman seek to know the unmanifested Brahman. Who with faith, themselves offer the oblations to the fire known as *Ekarshi*; to them alone whose mind is thus purified and who are therefore fit (to receive instruction) should one teach the knowledge of Brahman as also to those by whom is duly practised the vow of *Sirovratam* such being the well known Vedic vow among those who are of the Atharvana Veda.

तदेतत्सत्यमृषिरङ्गिराः पुरोवांच नैतदचीर्णव्रतोऽधीते ।

नमः परमऋषिभ्यो नमः परमऋषिभ्यः ॥ ११ ॥

This external *purusha* did the seer *Angiras* teach in

ancient times; none by whom the vow is not observed
studies this; prostration to the great sages, prostration
to the great sages.

Com.—This undecaying and true *purusha* did the seer,
known as Angiras, teach in ancient days to Saunaka
who had duly approached him and questioned him
(about this). The meaning is that, similarly, any other
also should teach the same to one who longs for bliss
and seeks emancipation and who with that end in view
has duly approached the preceptor. This knowledge in
the form of a book, no one who has not observed the
vow, studies; for it is knowledge, only in those who
observe the vow, that bears fruit. Thus ends the
knowledge of Brahman which has been handed down
from Brahma and the rest from preceptor to disciple.
Prostration to those sages Brahma and the rest, who
have directly seen the Brahman and realised him.
Prostration again to them; the repetition is both to
indicate great solicitude and the fact that the Munda-
kopanishad here ends.

Here ends the Second Part of
the Third Mundaka.

PRINTED BY G. A. NATESAN & CO., ESPLANADE, MADRAS.